Somewhere in Time . . .

Phoebe couldn't help noticing that something was very wrong: the way everyone was dressed like the cast of a Thanksgiving play, the horse and carriage, the buildings made of wood. . . . Unless I've landed in some bizarro Pilgrim party, she told herself, that demon brought me into another time zone—one that's not even close to Pacific Standard!

Suddenly it seemed as if everyone in the village was rushing over to gawk and gasp at the strange girl hiding behind the cart.

"See her belly?" an old woman said, scowling. "Pierced with a ring, it is. It is the mark of the devil, I say."

Phoebe glanced down. "My navel ring," she muttered under her breath.

"Witch!" the mob cried, closing in around her. "Witch! Witch!"

Phoebe felt the hair on the back of her neck stand up. If she remembered correctly, people in the past didn't exactly like witches.

In fact, they sometimes made a point of killing them.

D1366342

Charmed®

Published by Simon & Schuster

WHISPERS
FROM THE PAST

An original novel by Rosalind Noonan
Based on the hit TV series
created by Constance M. Burge

SIMON SPOTLIGHT ENTERTAINMENT
New York   London   Toronto   Sydney

First Pocket Pulse edition June 2000
First Simon Pulse edition August 2002
First Simon Spotlight Entertainment edition December 2004

S|S|E

SIMON SPOTLIGHT ENTERTAINMENT
An imprint of Simon & Schuster Children's Publishing Division
1230 Avenue of the Americas, New York, NY 10020

19 18 17 16 15 14 13 12 11 10

ISBN: 0-671-04165-7

WHISPERS
FROM THE PAST

CHAPTER 1

The warlock backed up against the brick wall.

He was cornered, trapped in a shadowed, narrow alleyway behind the colorful retail shops in San Francisco's popular North Beach district.

The man with the oddly glittering yellow eyes growled at Phoebe Halliwell and her sisters, Piper and Prue. Phoebe wanted to laugh. Like the guy had a reason to be mad at them! He was the one who had jumped down from a fire escape, grabbed Piper by the hair, and muttered something about the dark side.

When the creep crashed their party, the three sisters had been innocently making their way into the old warehouse that had been converted to a shopping mall. Prue had seen a pair

1

of boots she liked at a place called Kick in the Pants, but she had wanted a second and a third opinion before she laid out two hundred dollars for something she didn't really need.

"Honey, if you love them, you need them," Phoebe had told her, slinging an arm around Prue's shoulders as they'd cut down a narrow side street—a deserted narrow side street.

Phoebe had to admit that maybe her shortcut hadn't been such a great idea. Jeez, she thought. You head out for a pair of boots, you wind up with a hostile warlock in your face.

Not that fighting warlocks was anything new to Phoebe and her sisters. They were the Charmed Ones, three witches with special powers. Since they'd found *The Book of Shadows* in the attic of Halliwell Manor, the home they'd inherited from their grandmother, they had begun to learn the Craft.

The sisters made a pact to harm no one, as Gram would have wanted, and to use their powers for good. That included fighting off lots of evil beings, like this guy. They were getting pretty good at it, too. Phoebe was beginning to realize that as long as she and her sisters were together—as long as they had the Power of Three—nothing could stop them.

For the moment they were winning this battle as well. Piper, who'd gotten her hair out of the warlock's grip by stomping on his instep, now blocked the steep stairway that led to the alley. Prue stood in front of the street exit. Phoebe stood in front of the guy, so close she could reach out and peel the evil smirk off his face. They had him surrounded and he knew it.

Phoebe pushed up the sleeves of her favorite black leather jacket, ready to fight.

"I don't know why you're here," Prue told the warlock. "And I don't know where you come from. But you're going to be sorry you came." Her blue eyes flashed with anger as a strand of jet-black hair slipped down, touching her cheek.

"Really?" the warlock growled. "If you're trying to frighten me, you'll have to try harder. Much harder."

"Happy to oblige." There was no mistaking the mix of hatred and fierceness in Prue's voice.

All of Phoebe's senses were on alert, hypersensitive to the musty smell of the alley, the sight of the dirty wooden crates lining its sides, the buzz of cars and buses on the street at its other end, and the scuffling sound of shoes on cement as Piper stepped forward, slowly, cautiously. In tune with the moment, Phoebe felt her palms begin to sweat. Sure, there was a certain rush of adrenaline when facing a warlock. It was either fight like crazy or find yourself eating dirt. But even her free spirit couldn't ignore the danger element. This creep might wind up doing some serious damage to her or to her sisters.

Piper stepped forward again, closing the circle. The warlock lifted his hand. In it was a flash of silver—a dagger!

Phoebe felt every muscle in her body go taut. Where did that thing come from?

The warlock whipped his hand over his shoulder like a dart champion. Then, with his eyes dead-set on Phoebe, he thrust his hand forward and let the dagger go. Phoebe gasped as the silver blade sailed forward . . . coming right at her!

Phoebe closed her eyes. She couldn't help flinching, expecting the cold, sharp edge of the knife to slice through her leather jacket and T-shirt and flesh.

But she felt nothing.

Phoebe opened her eyes to find the dagger suspended in midair, just inches away from her chest. Behind it, the warlock was frozen in place, his face twisted in a sneer.

Phoebe knew Piper had used her power to freeze time.

"That was close," Prue said.

"You're telling me." Phoebe shuddered and wiped her palms against her jeans.

With a look of concentration and a wave of her hand, Prue used her power of telekinesis to knock the dagger out of the air. It clattered onto the cement at Phoebe's feet.

"Who *is* this guy?" Piper raked back her long brown hair, looking rattled. "You know, I think he blocked my powers for a minute. I kept trying to freeze him and I got zilch, nada."

"Creepy," Phoebe said, bending down to pick up the dagger.

The second she touched it, she felt its powers. Energy rippled from it into her hands. Holding on tight, she saw a vision unfold. That was Phoebe's gift: She saw visions of the future, of the past, and sometimes of worlds in between. Now she heard evil laughter. She saw a flash of light, then a swirl of green smoke, twisting, twirling in a vortex.

Two figures began to emerge beyond the green smoke.

Pop!

The picture in Phoebe's mind went blank. Confused, she stared down at the dagger.

"What is it, Phoeb?" Piper asked.

"Something's very wrong here," Phoebe answered. "I was starting to get a vision, but all of a sudden it just . . . ended. Like someone didn't pay the cable bill."

"What did you see?" Prue demanded.

Phoebe shrugged. "Just . . . I don't know. A lot of green."

"Green?" Piper squinted. "As in plants and trees?"

Phoebe shook her head. "More like green smoke."

"Kind of like a smoke screen?" Prue folded her arms and scowled at the frozen man. "So, even in a freeze you're blocking Phoebe's visions? You must be one powerful warlock."

"What are we going to do?" Piper asked nervously. "He's going to unfreeze any minute. And our powers—"

"Are *fine*," Prue said firmly. The eldest sister, Prue had a way of making things sound as if they were totally under control.

Still holding the cold dagger, Phoebe tried to think of a way to put the lid on this warlock. "There has to be a spell or *something* we could use. After all, he's just a warlock."

Piper's brows lifted. "*Just* a warlock?"

Phoebe sighed. Piper was probably the most cautious of the three sisters—sometimes too cautious.

"I mean, he's human, like us," Phoebe said, waving the dagger as she talked. "Just a man who practices evil witchcraft. And we've dealt with much worse."

"Plus, it's all of us against him," Prue said. "We have the Power of Three."

"Right," Phoebe said, turning the dagger to fend off the warlock. "Together, we can whip some major warlock bootie."

That made Piper smile—just for a minute— until they caught the flurry of movement that signaled the end of Piper's freeze. The warlock's evil grin faded. "What . . . ?" he muttered, confused. Then, when things registered, he let out a crackling roar.

"Is that a nasty sound, or what?" Piper said.

"People are so rude today," Prue agreed. "Whatever happened to manners?"

"Come on. I'm ready for you," Phoebe said, waving the dagger at him. A dark, engraved symbol flashed on the base of the dagger, catching her eye. What was that? It wasn't like any of the Wiccan symbols she'd ever seen—or even anything she'd encountered in black magic. What kind of a warlock was this guy? His powers were far beyond the human realm and far beyond those she'd seen in any other warlock. Way beyond—as if from another plane.

Duh! Phoebe thought. Of course! Maybe he wasn't human at all. Maybe he was a monster. Or a demon. Or a—

Whoa! The man launched a high kick at the dagger in Phoebe's hand. "Hey!" she cried. She took a step back against the brick wall. Kick averted. Danger coming right up.

"Change of plans," she shouted to her sisters. "I don't think he's a—"

"Brrrrraaaah!" the warlock raged, cutting her off.

"Oooooh. Someone isn't happy," Prue said dryly.

"Frustrated because you couldn't get this?" Phoebe asked, holding up the dagger with a taunting smile.

The warlock fixed Phoebe with a vicious stare. His yellow eyes seemed to penetrate her, making her shiver for a moment. Then he refocused on the dagger in her hand. Phoebe clutched it tightly as it went cold, then tickled her hand.

Something was happening.

As she watched in amazement, the dagger began to shimmer and break up into swirling particles. The particles flashed and whirled. Then the dagger disappeared. Her hand was empty.

"Okay," Piper said. "Now I'm scared."

Phoebe stared at the man, half-expecting to see the dagger reappear in his hand. What sort of weird powers did he have, anyway?

The girls continued to inch toward him, though now Phoebe wasn't sure of what they'd do with him once they'd trapped him. It wasn't as though anyone would wander into this alley to help them.

The warlock snatched a wooden crate from the floor of the alley and spun around, poised like a caged animal. He held the crate to his chest, then hoisted it through the air.

It sailed straight toward Piper.

"Make it stop!" Prue yelled to her sister.

Piper's face grew tight with concentration. Phoebe could tell that she was trying to stop the crate by freezing time—only Piper's freezing thing was, well, frozen.

Phoebe watched in shock and horror as the crate hit Piper, knocking her to the ground.

"No!" Prue cried. She rushed to Piper's end of the alley.

Phoebe looked from the man to her sisters. "Piper, are you okay?" she asked, trying not to let the warlock out of her sight.

Piper was nodding, trying to speak, but nothing came out of her mouth. Phoebe turned her head, concerned, and the warlock bolted. He streaked down the alley to the street exit, which was now wide open.

For a flash, Phoebe considered letting him go. Bad idea, she scolded herself. This guy was too powerful to be running loose in San Francisco. Might as well get the dirty work over with now.

"He's getting away!" Phoebe shouted to her sisters. She took off, giving chase. He was at the end of the alley now, glancing both ways down the street.

"No!" Prue's shout echoed down the alley. "Phoebe, stop! You can't do it alone."

Phoebe nearly skidded to a halt at the end of the alley. Prue had a bad habit of being right. Phoebe's power was the most passive of all the sisters'. Her visions wouldn't exactly help her if she got into hot water. Still, she couldn't just let that warlock—or whatever he was—get away!

Phoebe darted down the street, dodging an old man weighed down by grocery sacks.

There was no turning back now. The warlock was fast, but Phoebe was gaining on him.

Up ahead, the warlock shoved aside a baby stroller and knocked an orange crate from a sidewalk fruit stand. Phoebe kept her eyes fixed on him until he turned left, ducking out of sight.

Her heart pounded as she wove between an ice-cream cart and a hydrant like a slalom skier. No way was that monster getting away. Reaching the spot where he'd turned, Phoebe looked to her left and saw another alley, even darker than the first one.

The warlock was there, running past a cluster of Dumpsters. Phoebe lunged ahead. She couldn't lose him.

Then something started to happen. Phoebe stopped running and stood, panting, staring ahead. The warlock's skin was bubbling!

His entire body boiled into a mass of slimy, curdling green. His hair, his clothes, and his skin all began to melt away. Before Phoebe's eyes, his human disguise sloughed off.

The transformation complete, the creature swung around to stare back at her. Huge, bulbous brow ridges protruded from his skull above a gaping mouth of jagged, overlapping teeth. His skin was a series of bulging, oozing scars. A long, barbed tail had sprung from his lower back, and his feet had mutated into huge, clawed paws.

Phoebe's heart pounded in her ears as the truth hit her. This guy was evil incarnate: a gruesome, hideous demon.

This was worse than she'd thought. Demons had powers way beyond most warlocks and way, way, way beyond the scope of a newly practicing witch like Phoebe.

Okay, don't freak, Phoebe told herself. She had faced demons before with the help of her sisters.

Come to think of it, where were they now?

Stay cool, Phoebe thought. She checked out the dark alley behind the festering green demon. It was a dead end, blocked in by three brick walls. There were no doorways, no exits, no stairs to climb.

No way out for the screaming green monster, Phoebe thought. She folded her arms against the chill of the shadowed alley. All she had to do was keep him cornered until her sisters joined her. Piece of cake.

But the demon was off again, charging farther down the alley. Where's he running to? Phoebe wondered, staring into the shadows. There's only a brick wall back there.

But he was moving fast, his waxy green feet bouncing along the dirty pavement.

Okay, maybe he's a stupid demon, she thought, following him.

"Where do you think you're going?" she shouted.

"Want to catch me?" he called over his scarred green shoulder. "See if you can!"

"What am I, a three-year-old?" Phoebe snapped back at him. She frowned. He was a stupid, smart-aleck demon—the worst kind.

Picking up speed, Phoebe gritted her teeth and ran right at him. She was going to grab him by his pimply green neck and . . .

He ran farther. Phoebe couldn't believe it. He was going to slam into that wall!

Only, it wasn't a brick wall anymore. The air in front of the bricks and mortar was shimmering. The whole wall was fuzzy, moving like snowy reception on a broken television. As the demon reached it, Phoebe saw what he was doing. Somehow he was magically creating an opening in the wall—an escape hatch.

Well, it wasn't going to be that easy. Not with her on his tail—literally.

As he dived headfirst into the swirling hole, Phoebe reached in after him. "Gotcha!" she called, firmly grasping his tail. She wedged the toes of her boots against the base of the wall, leaned back, and pulled with all her strength. She needed to yank this sorry demon back into the alley.

"Whoa! What's going on?" Phoebe felt the shimmering wall begin to give way under her feet. She couldn't get any leverage.

She wasn't yanking the demon out of the hole, she realized. He was pulling her in! The wall began to disintegrate and swirl around them. Bricks were sucked into the hole as though they were dust particles in a giant vacuum. Phoebe could feel herself edging into the vortex, inch by inch.

I have to let go! she shrieked to herself. I have to get out of this hole!

But as the demon's tail slipped out of Phoebe's hands, she felt her feet skidding along the ground.

"Piper!" she cried. "Prue!" She wriggled and kicked and bucked against the incredible force.

It was too late. With each tug, she felt herself slipping out of the alley.

Twisting around, Phoebe caught a quick glimpse of brick wall and blue sky. Then everything was a dark, wavy blur as the black hole sucked her in.

CHAPTER 2

"I saw her turn down this way," Piper said, rushing into the alley. Her arm throbbed where the crate had hit her, but that didn't matter right now. Phoebe had split away from them and chased after the warlock. The whole thing made Piper totally nervous. "You heard her, didn't you, Prue? She was calling us."

Prue's dark hair flew back from her pale face as she stormed into the alley. "I heard her, Piper, but . . ." She marched ahead three more steps, then held up her arms in frustration. "Where is she?" Prue glanced around again. "I told her not to go. Why doesn't she ever listen?"

Piper knew that Prue wasn't really mad at Phoebe. She was just freaking out because it

14

looked as if Phoebe and the warlock had some-how disappeared.

"Phoebe!" Piper called, trying to push back the wave of panic that kept rising inside her. She plunged on into the shadows. "Where are you?"

"She's not here." Prue crossed her arms as she surveyed the alley. "And there's no way out of this smelly dead end. So, you tell me—where did they go?"

Piper squinted into the dark alley. There were no doors or windows, no fences to climb, just two Dumpsters and four stories of brick wall. "Up?" she suggested, pointing to the roof. "Do you think the warlock scaled a wall and carried Phoebe along?"

Prue frowned more deeply. "He's a warlock, not Spider-Man."

Piper cautiously peered into one of the Dumpsters, holding her breath against the stench. It was empty. Beside her, Prue coughed and slammed the door closed on the other Dumpster.

"Looks like today was trash pickup day," she said, wiping her hands on her jeans. "Lucky us. Otherwise we'd be sorting through a mountain of garbage, looking for—" Her voice broke with emotion. "*Why* didn't she wait? I told her to wait!"

"Prue . . ." Piper reproached her sister. Right now it didn't matter why Phoebe was lost. The only thing that mattered was finding her.

Backing away from the awful-smelling garbage bins, Piper noticed a dark heap at the end of the alley. It was a pile of . . . rags? Old papers?

Wait a minute. Was the pile smoking?

"What's that?" she asked, heading over to check it out.

"It's clothes or something," Prue said.

Leaning over the still-smoldering heap, Piper reached out to touch a fold of cloth. She jerked her hand back, gasping. It was hot to the touch.

Piper couldn't take her eyes off the folded clothes. They were covered in oil and soot, but the dirt and smoke couldn't disguise the garment that lay there. On top of the heap was a jacket—Phoebe's favorite black leather jacket.

"Phoebe," Piper whispered.

Sinking down beside her, Prue stared at the pile of clothes in disbelief. Her blue eyes flashed with terror as she studied them, shaking her head.

Using a pen from her pocket, Prue separated the items in the smoking heap. There was Phoebe's jacket, her jeans, her T-shirt, bra, and underwear, even her sneakers—all of the things Phoebe had been wearing, all of them caked with oil and soot.

Kneeling on the cold ground, Piper felt dread overwhelm her. "What does it mean?" she asked. "If her clothes are here, then where is she? What happened to her?" The thought of Phoebe, alone, naked, maybe caught in a spell cast by the warlock was too much to deal with.

It was *all* too much—the shadowed alley, the putrid smells, the cold pavement under her knees. Tears stung her eyes as Piper buried her head in her hands.

"She's gone, Prue," Piper said. She tried not to sob but quickly lost the battle. "Something really awful has happened to her."

"No!" Prue insisted. "Phoebe's okay. She's got to be okay. This is just some . . . some nasty trick. That warlock probably used a spell. And spells can be undone, right? We're the Charmed Ones. We undo spells all the time."

"*With* Phoebe," Piper said softly. "And she's gone." Piper swiped at a tear rolling down her cheek. "I'm scared, Prue."

Reaching down, Prue helped Piper to her feet. Through her tears, Piper saw the restrained expression on her sister's face, as if she were about to say something but was too afraid to articulate it. Instead, Prue pulled her sister close and hugged her hard.

"It's going to be okay," Prue said. "We will figure this out."

Piper squeezed her eyes shut, hoping against her better judgment that her older sister was right.

"Look, Phoebe's not dead," Prue said emphatically. "I mean, there's another explanation for

this. There's got to be. We just need to find out
what happened. Then we need to find Phoebe."

Brushing away tears with the back of one
hand, Piper took a deep breath. "It's not that
easy, Prue. I mean, where do you start looking
for someone who went up in smoke? It's like
searching for a needle in a haystack—a *smoking*
haystack. We'd probably have more luck finding that stupid warlock."

Piper noticed a flash in Prue's blue eyes.
Piper knew that look. It meant that her sister
had an idea.

Prue squatted down beside the pile of clothes.
"They've stopped smoldering, I think," she muttered. "Piper, give me your backpack," she
ordered.

"What for?" Piper slipped off her backpack
and handed it over. "What are you doing?"

"Collecting Phoebe's clothes," Prue said.
Gingerly, she picked up the jacket, then tried to
fold it as neatly as possible without getting too
much of the oily soot on her hands. "These
clothes may be the key to finding her." She
unzipped Piper's pack and shoved the leather
jacket inside. "Maybe we can use them to do a
spell to locate a missing person."

"I didn't think of that." Kneeling beside her
sister, Piper helped gather up the rest of
Phoebe's clothes. They were still warm. It felt
so awful, touching her grimy things, wondering where Phoebe was, hoping she was okay.

"We've got to get home to look in *The Book of Shadows*," Prue said, zipping up the backpack.

Yes, Piper thought, maybe the answer would be there. *The Book of Shadows* was full of illustrations and spells that had been passed down by the sisters' ancestors. It was started by a woman named Melinda Warren who had been burned as a witch in the 1600s. Many women in their family had used and recorded things in the book. It had been used last by Gram, the woman who'd raised Piper and her sisters.

"Have you ever seen anything about this in the book?" Piper asked. "Warlocks with the power to melt people? A spell that makes someone go up in smoke?"

"Not that I remember. But there's so much we haven't gotten to yet." Prue stood up and brushed off her hands. Piper noticed a smudge of soot on her cheek.

She reached over and gently rubbed it off with her thumb. "I almost hate to leave here," Piper said, hugging herself as she stared at the brick walls around her. "It's the last place Phoebe's been."

Something flickered in Prue's eyes. Was it fear? Piper wasn't sure.

"Prue, do you really think she's okay?" Piper had to ask.

"Absolutely." Prue slipped Piper's pack over her shoulder, looking as confident as ever.

Piper was sure she was only acting brave, but somehow it made her feel better.

"Phoebe is definitely okay," Prue told her sister. "And if that warlock did anything to hurt her, the two of us are going to collectively kick his sulfurous butt."

"Prue? Piper? Can you hear me?" Phoebe shouted. But she didn't hear her sisters' voices, only her own bubbling and reverberating as if she were talking underwater. She kicked and thrashed, feeling like a swimmer who couldn't find the surface. But it didn't seem to matter if she moved. She was caught in swirling mist, moving through a vortex. Like a bug in the wind, she had no choice but to go where the force took her.

All the while she sensed the demon's presence—his royal putridness. He was near, but where? All she could see were swirling colors, shadow and light. Why? Had he trapped her in some bizarro astral demon plane?

Phoebe really didn't know enough about these things to figure it all out. "Piper!" she yelled. "Prue!" The words bubbled around her, flat and dead. She knew her sisters couldn't hear her, and there was nothing she could do about it.

She glanced around and noticed an opening ahead. She was sailing right for it.

Suddenly the mists around her grew thicker,

blinding her. "Ow!" She slammed down on something hard. What was it? She gingerly lowered her hands and felt dirt, hard-packed dirt, beneath her.

The mist cleared from around Phoebe. She rubbed her eyes. She still felt a little dizzy, but she was relieved to be sitting on solid ground.

Actually, she realized, she was sitting in an alley. Definitely not the same one she was in before, unless the demon had turned all the brick buildings to wood. But at least this was real. Yes! Back on good old planet Earth.

Then she spotted him just a few feet away— the demon. He was holding his huge head in his clawed hands. Okay, Phoebe thought, time for a showdown with Mr. Green Slime.

She scrambled to her feet, but he was already up and running, bouncing down the alley toward the light at the end. "Hey!" she called after him. "This game of tag is really starting to irritate me!"

He lumbered to the mouth of the alley and scurried off into the sunlight. Phoebe followed. As she ran, she realized that the ground hurt her feet and she felt strangely cold, but she filed that away to deal with later.

She paused in the shadow at the end of the alley to peer out into the quiet street. Where was that demon? There was no sign of him anywhere. There weren't even any people in sight, only narrow clapboard houses with steep shingled roofs. Shivering in the cool breeze, Phoebe bit her lip and wondered how he could have slipped away so quickly.

The demon was gone. Disappeared. And she had no idea of where she was or why she was so cold.

Phoebe glanced down and— Hey! The demon wasn't the only thing that had vanished. Her clothes were gone, too. She was stark naked!

"Well, would you look at that!" Phoebe exclaimed aloud. She folded her arms to cover her chest and sidled over to a wooden cart to hide the rest. Now that demon had really annoyed her. Not only had he yanked her through that wall and dumped her who-knows-where, he had left her without a shred of clothing. She was really going to let him have it when she caught up with him. She wasn't quite sure *what* she was going to let him have, but that slimy green demon was going to pay.

Pressed against the cart, Phoebe noticed that it was loaded with a small basket of potatoes and a sack of something that looked like grain. Slung over the seat was a leather pouch on a belt. Hmm. She picked up the belt and looped it around her waist. Maybe this would cover some of the things that mattered, at least temporarily. After she'd fastened it around on the tightest notch, the belt still hung below her belly button, but for now it was the best she could do.

Okay, now she looked like a half-naked cowgirl.

Phoebe heard footsteps. She glanced left. Coming down the lane was a man with a sack slung over his shoulder. "Please don't notice me. Please don't notice me," she whispered.

From her hiding place, Phoebe studied the man. His shirt and pants were black—pretty standard. But his leather shoes definitely predated Doc Martens, and his hat was something off the *Mayflower*.

Okay, Phoebe thought, so he's making a fashion statement. But what exactly was he trying to say? She crouched even lower behind the cart as the man drew closer. His eyes were fixed on the ground, and he strode right by. She was safe.

But only for a moment. From the opposite direction came three women in severe black bonnets with dark, drab ankle-length dresses to match. Ugh. The last thing Phoebe needed was an encounter with the Nun Squad, especially when she just wanted to deal with the demon, find some clothes, and then get back home. If these chicks noticed her, things might get sticky.

Phoebe ducked down again until they'd passed by. Maybe I can find a clothesline to raid somewhere, she thought. Then I'll be able to get down to business. Phoebe peered at the women as they passed, through the spokes of the wagon wheel.

Wait a minute—a wagon wheel? Definitely not your everyday San Francisco hiding place. A whinnying sound met her ears. No, she thought. It couldn't be. She turned slowly to the right. Yup, it was—two horses hitched to the cart. How could she not have noticed them earlier?

Probably the whole being-naked thing, Phoebe reasoned. It was a little distracting.

But something was very wrong here, even more wrong than she had first thought. She pieced together all the information she had: the way everyone was dressed like the cast of a Thanksgiving play, the horse and carriage, the buildings made of wood. Phoebe bit her lower lip. Unless I've landed in some bizarro Pilgrim party, that demon brought me into another time zone—one that's not even close to Pacific Standard!

There was no use denying it: She'd gone back in time. Way back. That swirling vortex thingy must have been a time rift.

Phoebe had read about time rifts in *The Book of Shadows*. They were like waves that could transport you to the past or present. They were also seriously advanced magic—not something that she or her sisters had ever thought about trying to use.

"Who goes there?" called an angry male voice.

Phoebe felt goose bumps on the back of her neck as she spun around. A short, waxy-faced man in a broad-brimmed hat stood behind her. He stared at her with such astonishment, you would have thought *she* was the demon.

Phoebe crouched down behind the cart, but there was no point. She'd been discovered.

"Well, hello to you, too," Phoebe said with all the grace she could muster. She positioned her arms strategically to hide anything that might be on display. Talk about feeling exposed!

The man with the waxy face pointed directly at her. "I do believe the lady hath no clothes!" he announced in a loud voice.

No lie, Wax Man, Phoebe thought.

Immediately he was joined by the three women who had passed by and a couple who'd stepped out from the doorway of a nearby building. Two men in long leather aprons emerged from a place that looked like a stable. A man driving a horse cart stopped short as he turned onto the lane.

Suddenly it seemed as if everyone in the village was rushing over to gawk and gasp at the naked girl hiding behind the cart.

Why don't I just sell tickets, Phoebe thought, shivering as a cool breeze blew over her.

Was she supposed to explain to these people

that she was from another time and that she had
ventured here to pursue a demon? Not likely.

People in the crowd murmured and stared.
A few even giggled. Then an older woman
stepped forward and thrust a withered finger
toward Phoebe's stomach.

Phoebe swallowed hard. Uh-oh. This was
starting to get scary.

"See her belly?" The old woman scowled.
"Pierced with a ring, it is. It is the mark of the
devil, I say."

"Truly!" someone agreed.

"The devil, indeed!" Wax Man shouted.

Phoebe glanced down. "My navel ring," she
muttered under her breath. Hugging her chest
more tightly, she closed her eyes for a second
and wished she could be anywhere but here.
The expressions on the faces in the crowd
turned harder, their stares suddenly grim.

The old woman was still pointing, her wrinkled hand shaking with fervor. "The woman
bears a ring through her flesh, and yet she lives
and breathes!" she cried. "Truly, she must be a
witch!"

"A witch?" the murmur rippled through the
crowd.

Phoebe's mouth dropped open. What could
she say? Actually, I am a witch. But I'm a good
one. Really! It's not what you're thinking at all.

"Yes, yes, I see it!" another woman shouted.
"She must be a witch!"

Phoebe fell back against the cart as the crowd loomed large around her.

"Witch!" the mob cried, closing in around her. "Witch! Witch!"

Phoebe felt the hair on the back of her neck stand up. American history wasn't her strong point, but if she remembered correctly, the Puritans didn't exactly like witches. In fact, they made a point of killing them.

Suddenly she knew what that demon had been up to, bringing her here. She knew, and she didn't like it one bit.

CHAPTER
3

The sea of red, angry faces swam before Phoebe's eyes. Fear took over inside her. Her hands began shaking. Her fingers dug into the wood of the cart, trying to hold on.

But she couldn't fight the wave of terror. It swept through her, numbing her legs and arms until they were no longer under her control. She felt her knees give way. Everything went black. She collapsed, expecting to hit the cold, hard ground.

Instead, her landing was gentle and velvety. "Mmm . . ." she moaned, struggling to open her eyes.

When she did, a lean, handsome face filled the sky above her. Square jaw, high cheekbones, steely gray eyes. Definitely not a bad dream, she thought.

The earth shifted below her, and Phoebe's head fell back against something soft and warm. Hey, that wasn't the earth moving, she realized. It was the gorgeous guy lifting her, cradling her like a baby.

Phoebe closed her eyes for a second, hoping to shake off the dizzy feeling. Okay, a stranger with to-die-for good looks is holding me in his arms. She opened one eye for a quick peek, then closed it again. And I'm naked. Wrapped in a really soft cloak or something, but still pretty much top-to-bottom naked.

The stranger pushed through the crowd, carrying her toward his horse cart. "My sincerest apologies, especially to the ladies," the man spoke in a strong, confident voice. Phoebe could feel his chest vibrating under her ear when he spoke.

"This was not at all the way I had intended for the good folk of Salem to make the acquaintance of my dear sister, simple though she is." He swept past the three women dressed in black, who were contorting their necks to get a good view of Phoebe and the stranger.

Who was he talking about? Phoebe wondered.

"Simple she may be," the wax-faced man said. "Your sister is also quite naked, Mr. Montgomery."

Ahhh. So that's his name. Phoebe noted the information.

"Indeed, my good friend," Mr. Gorgeous Montgomery replied. He lifted Phoebe onto the flat seat of the cart and smoothed out a fold in the cloth around her, taking his time to see that she was securely wrapped. "My dear sister, are you ill? Where are your possessions? Your clothes?"

Realizing that she was part of this play, Phoebe stiffened. He needed an answer. They all needed a big fat answer, and they weren't going to buy the standard "The demon ate my homework" excuse.

Leaning forward to Mr. Montgomery, she whispered, "I was robbed."

"Robbed!" he repeated in a booming voice for all to hear.

A few women gasped. Then the crowd was hushed as all faces turned toward Phoebe. Feeling their eyes on her, she pulled the cloak tighter.

"My poor, dear sister." Mr. Montgomery buried his face in his hands for a moment, then glanced up at Phoebe. "After traveling so long and far to join me, it saddens me to know that conniving thieves took advantage of your generous, simple nature."

"Speaking of thieves," Wax Man piped up, "I'll have my belt back."

"Of course," Phoebe said. Standing on the

wobbly cart, she bit her lower lip as she struggled to keep her balance *and* keep her body hidden under the cloak. At last she slipped the leather belt and pouch down to her ankles and handed it to Wax Man. He held it in the air between two fingers, keeping it as far away from himself as possible. "Hey! I don't have cooties you know!" Phoebe defended herself.

"Where did she come from?" a man in the crowd growled. "There have been no ships in port for nearly a fortnight."

"She has been traveling over land," Mr. Montgomery explained smoothly. "From the colony of Jamestown. She was to marry a young man there, but alas, he was stricken with illness and passed during the winter months. She tried to stay on with the colony, however, I fear the good people of Jamestown could not tolerate her lapses in judgment."

"Aye. Perhaps we cannot tolerate her lapses in judgment, either," complained a woman in the crowd.

"And you shall not be asked to," Mr. Montgomery said, bowing to the woman. "Begging your pardon for any embarrassment you were caused. I am bringing my sister to the cottage. From this day forward I assure you she is under my care and protection. She will not be a burden to this colony."

"As you say, sir," the woman said with a deep nod.

It was quite a story, Phoebe had to admit, and Mr. Montgomery was quite a storyteller. As Phoebe watched him play to the crowd, she wondered why he would go to so much trouble for her, a complete stranger. A completely naked stranger. Wait, was *that* the reason?

The villagers stood by quietly as Mr. Montgomery climbed up beside Phoebe and took the reins. "Good day to you all," he called, and then they were off, bumping down the rutted lane in the open coach.

Phoebe was relieved to be away from the condemning eyes of the villagers. But as the cart left the small cluster of cabins and followed the trail into a dense wooded area, she found it hard to formulate a plan. Where was this guy taking her? And why? More important, how was she going to find that demon and make her way back home?

Her head was spinning again.

"We haven't had the honor yet," the man said, turning those killer gray eyes toward Phoebe. "I'm Hugh Montgomery. Dare I ask your name?"

"Phoebe Halliwell," she said. "That much I'm sure of."

"And where are you from, Phoebe Halliwell? I'll wager it isn't Jamestown."

Phoebe wondered how much she should tell him. Saying she was from the twenty-first century might not be such a good idea. "The truth is, everything's sort of hazy right now," she answered. Doing some quick calculating, she decided to stick with the robbery story. Hey, it had worked on the angry mob, right?

"My head still hurts," she said, rubbing her temples. "I must have gotten a pretty good whack when those robbers hit me."

" 'A pretty good whack'?" he repeated, as if he were trying to learn a foreign language.

"A bump on the head," she translated. She would have to remember that they spoke a little differently here.

"So it was truly robbers who stole your clothing?" he asked.

Phoebe nodded. "And ever since they hit me, my memory is hazy. I just can't think clearly right now."

"Perhaps you need rest," he suggested. "Rest and a cup of root tea."

"Whatever," Phoebe said. She paused. "You know, I appreciate the way you handled things back there in the village. But I have to ask, why did you do it—especially for a stranger? Those people could have turned on you. They might have stoned you or something."

He smiled. "People are not stoned in Salem. We have far more civilized means of punishment when necessary."

Phoebe's breath caught in her throat. "Salem?" she echoed. "I'm in Salem?"

He nodded. "Salem Village, Massachusetts."

Phoebe swallowed. "And, um, what year is it, please?"

"Sixteen seventy-six." Hugh answered.

Phoebe felt the hair on the back of her neck stand up. Salem in the late 1600s? It was practically the witch-killing capital of the world then! Suddenly things were falling into place. The demon had brought the witch to the witch killers. If Phoebe hoped to survive long enough to get home, she'd better watch her step.

"Are you all right?" Hugh asked. "Your face suddenly paled."

Phoebe nodded. "I guess I still feel a little . . . strange." More like terrified, she added silently. But it was better if Hugh didn't know that, so she steered the conversation back to her earlier question.

"Why did you help me?" she asked again. "Why take the risk?"

Hugh's smile faded as he stared off in the distance. "A few months ago someone saved me—the Widow Wentworth. She gave me food and a place to stay when I had nowhere else to turn. I shall never forget that act of kindness and have sworn to do the same whenever I meet someone in need."

So it's not just a physical thing, Phoebe thought, warming to Hugh. This Good Samaritan had potential. Too bad he lived in the wrong century.

"Did you ever get a chance to thank this Mrs. Wentworth?" she asked.

Hugh smiled again. "I thank her every day. It's her cottage I am taking you to. I tend to the animals and garden for her in exchange for food and a pallet to sleep on in the barn."

The cart bumped over a rut in the road. Readjusting her position on the seat, Phoebe tugged the cloak tighter. "Oh, great. Another stranger in her home. I bet old Widow Wentworth is gonna love me."

"Indeed," he said. "She is a kind and generous woman."

Soon Phoebe noticed the trees giving way to a clearing.

"That's her cottage, there," Hugh said, nodding to a modest log cabin with a thatched roof. A small barn stood off in the distance, next to a field that had been recently plowed.

The horse brought them to the side of the cottage. Hugh jumped to the ground and hurried around to help Phoebe out of the cart, treating her as if she were a piece of breakable china. Not that she minded—she was just a little surprised. After all, in the twenty-first century, some guys' idea of romance was a playful punch in the shoulder.

Hugh grabbed a covered basket from the back of the cart and led the way to the cottage door. He knocked. Phoebe stood up straight.

Prepare to meet the widow, she coached herself. But no one answered.

"She must be out," Hugh said, gently pushing the door open. "Please . . ." He held a hand out for her to enter first.

Cautiously, Phoebe stepped into the shadows. The room was dark and smelled of wood smoke and honeysuckle. Pleasant smells. In front of her she saw polished wood furniture carved with decorative flowers. A colorful rag rug lay on the dirt floor. The room was cozy and welcoming. There was a sink in the corner, but no faucet, which meant no running water. No indoor plumbing. There also weren't any microwaves or stoves or ovens. No phones. Definitely no takeout. Hmmm. This was going to be like camping. Sort of.

Hugh took some neatly wrapped packages from the basket and set them on the pine table. "Dry goods for the widow," he explained. "Ribbons, buttons, thread, and a length of calico."

Phoebe seated herself on a wooden chair and looked down at her feet.

"Are you cold?" Hugh asked. "I'll start a fire."

Phoebe nodded at Hugh. It could have been worse, she figured. At least she didn't time-rift into the Arctic. From the planting and the mild weather, she guessed that it was springtime here in Salem, just as it was back in San Francisco.

Hugh pushed another log onto the fire. "That'll get the kettle to boil," he said, brushing off his hands. "I'll be outside splitting more wood. Stay here and rest a while. The others shall be back soon."

"The others?" Phoebe asked.

"The widow and her daughter," Hugh said as he headed out the door.

Pulling her feet onto the chair, Phoebe stared up at the thatched roof. She groaned. "What am I *doing* here?"

She leaned forward, plunking her head and arms on the table. One arm accidentally knocked into a clay bowl, which clanked. "Don't break the widow's china," she scolded herself.

She peered into the bowl, which stood alone on the large pine table. Inside was a charm—a gold piece in the shape of a crescent moon. Curious, Phoebe picked up the charm and— *wham!*

Her thoughts spilled into another place and time as a vision took over her consciousness.

Fire. The flames were everywhere, shooting up to the sky.

They danced and waved, wrapping a woman in their wispy embrace. She was young, blond, beautiful. A steely courage shone in her eyes. She was murmuring something. What was it? Around the woman's neck Phoebe saw the charm, the crescent moon gleaming in the flames.

A shudder rippled through Phoebe's body as she recognized the woman. It was her ancestor Melinda Warren. She had once appeared as a ghost to help the Charmed Ones, and Phoebe had seen many of her spells in *The Book of Shadows*. Melinda was the original witch in Phoebe's bloodline.

The vision ended as the flames rose to a towering height around Melinda. Melinda Warren had been burned at the stake in Salem in 1654. Just twenty-two years earlier, Phoebe remembered. So what was her charm doing in this cottage?

Had the Widow Wentworth had a hand in Melinda Warren's death?

CHAPTER 4

Ï feel so guilty," Piper said as she followed her older sister through the doorway of Halliwell Manor. The old, heavy door swung shut behind them. It closed with a click. The sound usually made Piper feel safe. Today it sounded so final. "It's like we just left Phoebe behind."

"We are taking action," Prue said firmly. "We are going to march up to the attic, find a spell in *The Book of Shadows*, and get our sister back. We're taking the bull by the horns. Or, actually, the warlock by the horns."

"I'm glad someone's in control." Piper's boots clicked on the shiny hardwood floors. Since their grandmother had left them Halliwell Manor in her will, the sisters had done their best to keep it sparkling, from the colorful stained-glass windows to the elegant chandelier. The sprawling Victorian had warmth, charm, and, as the girls had discovered, magic lurking in every corner.

Wasting no time, Prue and Piper threw off their coats, hung them on the rack, and headed up the wide, sweeping staircase. On the second story was a more modest staircase that led straight up to the attic. Inside the attic, as always, lay *The Book of Shadows*.

Piper crossed the dusty room to light some candles. Kneeling beside a low, round table, she struck a match and touched the wicks. The flames cast dancing glimmers of light over the raw wood and exposed beams of the attic. Sometimes the girls used candles for their spells. Now Piper lit them, hoping that the light would ward off the horrible chill she'd been fighting ever since Phoebe had disappeared.

"Okay, let's see." Prue was already leaning over *The Book of Shadows*, flipping through its ancient pages. "We have a spell to chase away rats. A chant for the summer solstice—put that on your calendar."

"Anything about retrieving a vanished sister?" Piper swallowed hard against the lump in her throat. Though she was tempted to join Prue at the book, she made herself sit down on the couch. When Prue was in command mode, she didn't appreciate being crowded.

"Give me a minute," Prue said, running her

finger down a page. She flipped a few pages ahead, frowning.

Piper bit her lower lip pensively. Over the past year she'd spent hours combing through *The Book of Shadows,* reading and studying. But it wasn't always easy to find what you were looking for. Consulting it wasn't like punching in a keyword for a computer search or looking up a term in an encyclopedia.

"Whoa!" Prue cried suddenly. "I think I've got something here. It's a tracking spell."

Piper stood to read over Prue's shoulder.

"Yes! This is it!" Prue pointed to a series of lines scrawled in an old-fashioned handwriting. "It's perfect. Let's see what we need." She read from *The Book of Shadows:*

> "A trace of paternity,
> Clothing so dear,
> A lock of hair
> To track far and near."

Piper counted off the items on her fingers. "A Dad thing, Phoebe's clothes, and her hair. How are we going to get that if she's not here?"

Tapping the book, Prue paused thoughtfully. "Let's see. . . ." She raised her hand to point downstairs. "Her hairbrush! It must have a few strands of Phoebe's hair in it."

Without another word the two sisters hurried

down to the second story. While Prue headed
toward Phoebe's bedroom, Piper went down to
the vestibule, where she'd dropped her backpack on the way in. Looping the strap over her
arm, she ran back up the stairs. She checked her
watch as she tore down the hall to Phoebe's
room. Three hours till the Saturday evening rush
was on at P3, Piper's new club. She'd have to
start getting ready to go, *if* she was going. It was
awful to have to be responsible for something
when your whole world was falling apart.

"I got the clothes," Piper said breathlessly.

Prue stood at Phoebe's dresser, sifting
through a stack of magazines. "And I have the
hair," she said, nodding toward Phoebe's hairbrush on the bed. "But the paternity thing
throws me. I mean, we don't have anything
from Dad. Why would we?"

"Well, obviously *you* wouldn't," Piper told
her sister. "You probably burned all his stuff
years ago."

"I didn't burn it," Prue argued. "I just never
saved anything."

The subject of their father was a sore point,
especially between Prue and Phoebe. As far as
Prue was concerned, he was a nonperson. He
had walked out of the Halliwell girls' lives
when they were very young, so Prue had written him out of her life entirely. But Phoebe had
always argued that Prue was wrong about
their dad.

Piper tried to stay out of their disagreement, although she occasionally found herself missing their dad, wishing she could connect with him.

"Okay, Piper. I'm reading the look on your face. You have something of Dad's, don't you?" Prue challenged.

Piper smirked.

"What is it?" Prue demanded.

"I *had* a photo of him as a teenager. But I gave it to Phoebe and—"

"And she never gave it back," Prue finished for her. Frustrated, she smacked Phoebe's brush against her hand. "We are so close to getting this spell done and finding Phoebe. Leave it to Dad to screw things up all over again!"

"Okay, okay, let's stay calm here and think." Piper sank onto Phoebe's bed. "Maybe there's a picture of him in one of the family photo albums."

Prue shook her head. "Mom got rid of those."

Piper held up her hand. "Wedding ring? Jewelry? Letters?"

Prue kept shaking her head. "Dad didn't write us any letters, remember?"

"There's got to be something." Piper's eyes wandered over the ticket stubs tucked into the frame of Phoebe's mirror. They were mostly tickets from dates to shows, amusement parks, and football games.

Football! Piper sprang to her feet. "I've got it!"

Prue watched as she opened the door of Phoebe's wardrobe and reached up to a box on the top shelf.

"I saw her pull this out of her trunk of stuff in the attic." Piper lifted a football out of the box. "This belonged to Dad. It was autographed by Johnny Unitas, the Golden Arm."

Cocking one brow, Prue eyed the football. "Right now I don't care if it's autographed by Elvis. If it belonged to Dad, we're using it." She tucked the football under her arm and grabbed the hairbrush. "Let's go," she said, heading toward the attic.

"Right behind you," Piper answered.

In the attic they began assembling the ingredients of the spell on the low table. Piper chose a wide, shallow ceramic bowl to hold the ingredients while Prue pulled a tangled mass of hair from Phoebe's hairbrush. She lined the bowl with Phoebe's soiled leather jacket, then placed the wad of hair on top. Once the football was nudged under the collar of the jacket, they were ready to begin.

Piper felt herself tense with urgency and anticipation. Would this spell bring Phoebe back? No, it was only supposed to help them locate her, but it was a start. It *had* to work.

Her heart was beating hard in her chest as she joined hands with Prue. It didn't feel the same without Phoebe completing the circle, but they pushed on.

"Okay." Piper's voice was solemn. "Let's recite the whole spell."

Together, they chanted:

> "A trace of paternity,
> Clothing so dear,
> A lock of hair
> To track far and near.
> Find our Phoebe,
> Point the way.
> Track her spirit,
> Find her today."

Piper glanced across the table at Prue's shadowed face. Nothing had happened. Did they do something wrong?

"Let's repeat the last part," Prue said.

" 'Find our Phoebe,' " they chanted in unison. " 'Point the way. Track her spirit . . .' "

A clean, soft wind blew through the attic.

" 'Find her today,' " the sisters finished chanting.

The wind swirled around the objects in the bowl. The football tilted up on one end, then balanced in the wind, spinning wildly. The jacket rose high above the table, then came alive, as if worn by an invisible mannequin. The sleeves flapped madly, pointing in every direction. Was the jacket pointing the way to Phoebe?

The ball of Phoebe's hair floated into the air, then burst into flames. The smell stung Piper's nose, and she pressed her sleeve to her face. Across the table Prue coughed, waving the smoke away.

Just as suddenly as it had kicked up, the wind died down. The jacket fell into the bowl, and the football rolled to its side and bounced onto the floor.

"What did that mean?" Piper asked, backing away from the odd display.

Prue immediately consulted *The Book of Shadows*. "Okay, it says the clothing may point the way, in one clear direction."

"But it didn't," Piper observed. "That jacket pointed north, south, east, west, and everywhere in between."

"Which means . . ." Prue consulted the book again. "It means that the person being tracked is not near. Right here it says, 'If the clothing dances indecisively, the spell reveals that the dear one's soul is far, far away.'"

Piper sank down onto the hard attic floor and pulled the football into her lap. A wave of nausea washed over her. "Tell me that doesn't mean what I think it means," she said quietly.

"What about the burning hair?" Prue said, flipping to the next page in the book. "That's got to mean something."

"Isn't fire usually a bad sign?" Piper asked.

When Prue didn't answer, Piper turned toward her sister. "Prue, what is it?"

Tears glimmered in Prue's blue eyes as she stared down at the book.

"What does it say, Prue?" Piper dropped the football and went to slip an arm around her sister's shoulders. "Tell me."

Prue shook her head furiously, swallowing back a sob. "It doesn't say anything. It's just . . . I mean, what if Phoebe is . . ."

"No," Piper snapped, shaking her sister by the shoulders. "No way. It can't be. Right? Right?"

But Prue didn't answer. She just closed her eyes. A single tear rolled down one ivory cheek.

Biting her lower lip, Piper refused to say the word that Prue had been avoiding. Neither of them could say it.

But they were both thinking it.

Dead. What if Phoebe was dead?

CHAPTER
5

The vision of Melinda Warren vanished, leaving Phoebe shaking. She dropped the half-moon charm back into the clay bowl and buried her face in the soft cloak enveloping her.

What did the vision mean? If this was 1676, Melinda had been dead for twenty-two years. So why did the charm touch off such a strong vision? Phoebe's visions always came for a reason. They usually meant she was supposed to do something about whatever she saw. So what was she supposed to do about this one?

Phoebe was still trying to figure out the vision when the door swung open and a child's laugh floated in.

"I told you, Mama," the young voice

chirped. "I can pick more wildflowers than anyone. And the egg in my pocket didn't get smashed at all. Not even when I ran."

Straightening, Phoebe was surprised to see a little girl who couldn't have been more than five enter the house. A woman who seemed close to Phoebe's age followed behind. Both were blond, fine-boned, and bright as a ray of sunshine. Phoebe blinked. This young mother couldn't be the Widow Wentworth, could she?

Somehow Phoebe had expected an arthritic, snaggletoothed hag, not someone so young and gorgeous.

"It's luck that saved the egg, not skill," the woman said. She glanced up and noticed Phoebe.

"Oh, goodness, did we wake you? Hugh told me you were in need of rest, and here we come bustling in." She hurried over to Phoebe. "I'm Prudence Wentworth, and this is my daughter, Cassandra."

Phoebe smiled. Yup. This is the widow all right. Funny, she's got the same name as Prue. "My name is Phoebe Halliwell," she introduced herself.

"Is it true about the robbers?" the little girl squeaked. "Truly, did they take all your clothes?"

"Cassandra," the woman said firmly, "back to the henhouse to collect the rest of the eggs."

"Yes, Mama," the little girl said obediently,

but her curious eyes never left Phoebe as she backed out the door and ran off.

"My apologies. My daughter is very inquisitive," Prudence explained. "You've suffered a terrible misfortune, but you are welcome here. Are you hungry? Or would you like a cup of tea to warm you?"

"Tea would be wonderful," Phoebe said as the woman picked up the clay bowl and took a moment to touch the charm inside. "That's lovely," Phoebe said, seizing the opportunity. "I mean, the charm. Where did you get it?"

Prudence stared off sadly. Turning away from Phoebe, she placed the bowl and charm on a side table, between two candles.

That almost looks like a witch's altar, Phoebe thought.

"The charm belonged to my mother," Prudence finally answered.

Her mother? Melinda Warren was her mother? Is it possible? Phoebe wondered. She ran the numbers in her head. If Prudence was born sometime before Melinda was killed, in 1654, that would make Prudence at least twenty-two, and that would make her Phoebe's ancestor—and Prue's namesake!

But maybe Prudence was lying about where she got the charm. Phoebe couldn't be sure. The big family reunion would have to wait until she was.

"This should last you through tomorrow,"

Hugh said, stomping in with his arms full of wood. He placed it beside the hearth. "Ah, I see you two have acquainted yourselves. I'll make us some tea." Using a forked wooden stick, he lifted the kettle from its spot over the fire and lowered it to the dirt floor.

"Not for me, thank you," Prudence said quickly. "Forgive me, but I am sick to death of root tea."

"But you must," he insisted. "I won't let you fall ill like the others."

"You are too kind, Mr. Montgomery," Prudence said.

He crossed the room and touched her hand gently. "I disagree. It is you who are most deserving," he told Prudence.

Hel-lo! Major romance vibe here, Phoebe realized. Then she frowned. Wait a minute. Weren't those gray eyes sparkling for me just a little while ago?

She took a deep breath, trying to rethink things. Maybe she'd been wrong about Hugh being interested in her.

Still, Phoebe wasn't usually mistaken about these things. When it came to love vibes, she prided herself on being tuned to the right frequency.

Noticing that Phoebe was observing the exchange, Prudence blushed and stepped away from Hugh. "Look at you, wrapped in Hugh's cloak, poor dear. Truly, there must be something in my trunk that would fit you. I shall find you a dress at once."

Hugh clasped Prudence's hand, pulling her back to his side. "I told Phoebe you were a generous soul, especially toward unfortunates who have nowhere to go. Phoebe is one such person. Could you find it in your heart to let her stay for a while? She might earn her keep by doing a few chores around the house."

"Yes, of course. We would never turn away a soul in need," Prudence said, her blue eyes alight with concern. Something about those blue eyes stirred feelings in Phoebe. They were so much like her sister Prue's eyes—smart, calm, caring. It made Phoebe wish more than ever that she could be back home.

"First things first," Prudence said. "I must fetch Phoebe a dress." She disappeared through a doorway toward the back of the common room.

Whistling softly through his teeth, Hugh set out some clay mugs and poured water from the kettle. Then he shook an odd assortment of dried scraggly twigs onto a piece of thin cloth and tied the cloth into a tiny sack.

"What are you making?" Phoebe asked.

"Root tea for Prudence," he said, dunking the sack into one of the mugs. "Would you like some?" An unpleasant scent arose as the roots steeped. It reminded Phoebe of wet socks.

"No, thanks. Regular tea is just fine for me."

"Prudence needs her root tea," Hugh said, taking a pinch of ground tea leaves from a small cloth sack. "There's been a dreadful sickness in a nearby village, and Prudence, who often tends the sick, was exposed to it. Root tea wards off the sickness."

If the smell doesn't make you sick first, Phoebe thought.

Hugh placed a mug of regular tea in front of her, and Phoebe adjusted the cloak so that she could slip one hand out to lift her cup.

As she moved she noticed that Hugh's eyes were all over her, and his mouth curved in a slight grin.

"My cloak has never been so happy," he said, "covering such precious things."

Raising one eyebrow, Phoebe leveled a skeptical look at him. The guy was totally flirting with her! What was his deal? Was he Prudence's main squeeze or wasn't he?

"I've found two dresses that might fit you, but you must choose between them," Prudence announced, appearing in the doorway. "Come and see."

With a stern look at Hugh, Phoebe stood up and wrapped the cloak so tightly she nearly had to waddle into the back room. It was one thing to fall into the arms of a steely-eyed rescuer. It was something else to move in on another woman's man, especially when that woman might be your ancestor.

Inside the back room, Prudence had laid out two dresses—one black and gray, the other a navy so dark that it might as well have been black. Drab or drabber? Phoebe thought, but finally she agreed with Prudence that the navy suited her better.

Prudence slipped out and returned with the kettle and a pitcher. Mixing the steaming water with cold water in a wide bowl, Prudence said, "You can use this to wash up."

"Thank you," Phoebe said. "For everything."

"You're quite welcome," Prudence assured her. "I'll be back to help you with the dress in a few moments."

Phoebe picked up the wash rag Prudence had left her and began washing the dust off her naked body. She'd gotten pretty gritty crouching there in the middle of the village—another bone to pick with the demon when she caught up with him.

Somewhat cleaner, Phoebe examined the clothing Prudence had laid out on the bed. There was a camisole and a long petticoat, both made from coarse muslin, and thick wool stockings. Oh, well, they might be scratchy but they were definitely underwear.

She put on all the items, then slipped the navy dress over her head. Phoebe stared down at herself, puzzled. The dress fit just fine around her shoulders but was rather wide at the waist.

Had Prudence worn this dress when she was pregnant with Cassandra? Great, Phoebe thought, maternity wear!

The door to the back room opened then, and Prudence came in, a needle and thread in one hand.

"Turn around," she said with a smile. "I'll take in the waist a bit."

"Thanks," Phoebe said. She turned around and grabbed hold of the thick wooden bedpost to steady herself.

Prudence gasped. "What happened to your fingers?" she asked.

"My fingers?" Phoebe let go of the bedpost and studied her fingertips. They seemed perfectly normal to her.

"No, the other side." Gently, Prudence turned over her hands. "Your fingernails are bleeding."

For a second Phoebe didn't get it. Then she realized. Her manicure! No one here polished their fingernails. Prudence had never seen shiny, bright red nails.

"They're not bleeding," Phoebe assured her. "They're . . . painted." But Prudence seemed baffled, so she improvised. "I was helping to paint a door red and got paint all over my hands. It washed off my skin but not my nails."

Prudence stared at her blankly. "Are you sure it doesn't pain you?" she asked.

"Positive," Phoebe assured her. She made a mental note to keep her hands hidden around the other villagers.

"Very well," Prudence said. "Let me help you with your dress then."

As Prudence took a few tucks in the waist of the dress she chatted about Cassandra and the huge help that Hugh had been since he'd arrived in Salem.

Clean and clothed, Phoebe began to feel better. She'd been lucky to connect with Prudence, who struck her as a warm, capable woman. Are you, like, my great-great-great-great-grandmother? Phoebe wondered as Prudence struggled to twist Phoebe's hair into a bun.

Phoebe wanted so much to believe it was true. For one thing, it would mean that Prudence was a witch, too. She'd know how to navigate the hostile villagers. And for another—Phoebe's eyes widened at the thought—*The Book of Shadows* would have been passed down to Prudence from Melinda. It would be right here in this house!

Phoebe felt her heart beat faster. Maybe she'd be able to get herself out of this mess, after all.

"There," Prudence said, putting down the brush. "Your hair is neat again, and the dress looks fine on you. Is there anything else you need?"

Just some help decimating a demon, Phoebe

answered silently. She thought for another moment. If she revealed her true identity and told Prudence all about the demon, Prudence could definitely help. Maybe she knew a spell that could whack that demon and send Phoebe rifting home.

"There's something you need to know," Phoebe said, her heart racing with excitement as she sat down on the bed, facing Prudence. "It's about me . . . who I am."

Prudence seated herself beside Phoebe. "Yes, Phoebe?"

Where do I start? Phoebe wondered, staring into Prudence's curious blue eyes.

"It's this thing about the robbers," Phoebe began.

Prudence cocked her head to one side, listening.

"I'm not really—" Phoebe stalled in midsentence.

I can't do this! I shouldn't be saying this. What if Prudence is your typical Salem Puritan—the kind who believed witches deserve to be killed?

"Please, go on," Prudence said, squeezing her shoulder gently. "Don't be frightened."

But Phoebe couldn't. Instead, she touched her forehead, muttering, "I was just going to say, I'm not really sure of all the details of my past, maybe because of this bump on my head. I mean, it's scary, but while I'm sorting everything out, it really helps to know that I can stay here. Thank you."

"You are most welcome," Prudence said, patting Phoebe's shoulder. "And you may stay as long as you like. I think we're going to become good friends, Phoebe Halliwell."

Don't get too attached, Phoebe thought, because if things go according to plan, I'm out of here on the next time rift.

"It must be hard to lose your memory of the past," Prudence went on sympathetically. "Especially since it is the actions in our past that shape our future."

Phoebe sat up straighter at that. She'd seen enough time travel movies to know that Prudence was right. She knew what could happen if she made the wrong move: She could change the course of the future—the future that her sisters were living in right now!

Her sisters. She wished they were here to help her. But they weren't. And with one wrong move, she might obliterate their very existence!

CHAPTER
6

The scent of honeysuckle and new grass filled the air. In the distance, birds chirped as Phoebe rolled over. All signs pointed to a beautiful spring morning.

Ouch. This was definitely not her own bed. What was she sleeping on—a sack of corn?

Opening her eyes, she remembered just how far from home she was. "Phoebe, you're not in Kansas anymore," she muttered as she propped herself up on one elbow. "You're in Prudence Wentworth's bedroom, sleeping on a straw mattress, in another century."

Moving her feet under the blanket, Phoebe wished she were home between the crisp sheets of her own bed, but she had a long way to travel before that could happen. First she had to find that demon and banish him. The fact that he'd managed to strand her in the past was proof that he was major danger. Plus if he'd yanked her out of her own time, he'd definitely try to block her way back, unless she dealt with him first. Only then could she head home—if home still existed. No pressure, she thought as she stretched her legs and yawned.

Phoebe noticed that the two beds across the room—the simple wood-framed bed where Prudence slept and the small child's bed that Cassandra used—were empty. This was her chance.

The night before, as she was falling asleep, Phoebe had thought of a surefire way to confirm that Prudence was who she claimed to be: find *The Book of Shadows* in the house. If Prudence was Melinda Warren's daughter, the book had to be there.

Quickly she slipped out of bed to search. The dirt floor was damp and cold, and she hopped from one foot to another, shivering. Finally she grabbed a shawl from the edge of Prudence's bed and wrapped it around her shoulders. Lifting the mattress, she looked under and around the bed. Nothing. She moved on to a chest of drawers. She was lifting a stack of linens out of a drawer when she heard voices in the other room.

"Phoebe?" Prudence called.

The blood rushed to Phoebe's face. She

quickly tucked the linens back into the drawer, closed it, and spun around.

"Coming!" she called back. She'd have to search for the book another time.

"Good morning to you," Hugh's voice boomed cheerfully.

Phoebe, clothed once again in Prudence's dress, stepped out into the common room. Hugh sat by the fire, sipping a cup of tea. Cassandra sat at the table, quietly rolling a tangle of wool yarn into a ball while her mother opened a steel grate and removed two thick slabs of bread that had been toasting on the fire.

"I've already fed the chickens, harvested the corn, and milked the cows," Hugh added, winking at Phoebe. "All before you opened your brown eyes."

The cocky grin on his face annoyed Phoebe. He was on the verge of flirting with her again—this time right in front of Prudence!

Choosing to ignore him, Phoebe turned to Prudence, who was setting out a plate of toast and a baked apple for her. "He's joking, isn't he?" Phoebe asked as she sat down and bit into a thick piece of toast. "You don't really have cows, do you?"

"We do," Prudence said without a hint of a smile. "But the corn won't be harvested until July or August." She held up a pitcher and peered inside. "We need more water," she sighed.

"Prudence, sit down," Hugh said gently. "Finish your root tea. Phoebe can fetch the water."

"There are plenty of chores for Phoebe to do," Prudence snapped. "And sleeping the morning away is not one of them."

Whoa, Phoebe thought. That was a big change from yesterday's "You need your rest" slogan.

"Mmm! I can geck wadder," Phoebe said over a mouthful of toast. She wasn't sure why Prudence was in such a bad mood this morning, but she didn't want to make it any worse than it already was. She swallowed her toast. "Why don't I just take this to go," she declared. She picked up a half-slice and dropped it into the pocket of her apron. No one said a word as she picked up two wooden buckets and headed out the door.

Outside the sun was already warming the damp earth. Phoebe took two steps, paused, then headed back to the cabin. Pushing the door open, she called out, "Okay, where do I get the water from?"

"The creek," Hugh answered. "Go past the chicken coop, right at the barn, down the hill, and over the rocks."

"Right," she said, backing out a second time. Man! This Colonial thing definitely had its glitches.

Hugh's directions were easy to follow, and Phoebe was able to finish her toast as she made her way down the hill. But once the buckets were filled with water they were incredibly heavy. She struggled up the hill, her hands hurting, water sloshing onto the hem of her dress. The muscles in her arms were beginning to ache when a sound came from behind her.

Glancing over her shoulder, Phoebe saw him—the hideous demon who had dragged her to this place. He stood a few feet behind her, his gruesome green skin oozing in the sun.

Phoebe dropped the buckets and stumbled backward.

"I scared you," he said with a slobbery smile.

"Yeah, well, it's rude to sneak up on people while they're fetching water," she said. She rolled her own eyes at her words. Oh, that would really wound the demon.

The truth was, she *was* scared and quaking in her boots. But this was the chance she'd been waiting for, the opportunity to banish the demon forever. Too bad she wasn't ready. She didn't have a spell or a curse or even a stick to fend him off with.

"Don't be afraid," the demon growled. His putrid flesh quivered as he spoke. "I'm not going to hurt you. At least, not right now. I have a long-term plan that's far more effective."

"I'll bet you do," Phoebe said.

"I'm planting the seeds even now," he explained. "Seeds that will take root and grow into a tangled, poisonous vine. A vicious thing that will bring pain and torture to you and all future generations of your family." He paused, letting his words sink in. "Before I am through, you will all be creatures of evil!"

Immediately, Phoebe thought of her sisters. And her mother. And Gram. Could this lowlife demon actually do that? Did he have the power to warp generations of women in her family?

"In the end, I *will* destroy you," he promised. "Slowly. Thoroughly."

Fighting off a shiver of fear, Phoebe stepped back. She wasn't going to be stupid enough to underestimate him a second time.

A low growl emerged from somewhere deep inside the demon, making Phoebe's heart thud in her chest. He pointed a twisted green finger at her. With a whoosh, a line of fire shot straight at her feet. She leaped backward, lifting her skirt. The flames had missed her, but she could feel the supernatural warmth of them through the leather of Prudence's boots.

"I thought you said you weren't going to be any trouble today," she reminded him.

"I lied." With that he pointed beyond Phoebe, to the top of the hill. Like a marksman he shot a line of fire into a haystack by Prudence's small barn.

Phoebe watched in horror as the flames caught and immediately shot up, swallowing the small mound of hay. She ran up the hill, as a small bundle of embers separated from the heap, quickly becoming airborne in the morning breeze.

The wind fed the flames, rolling the embers over the dirt—right toward the barn.

Phoebe froze, then ran back for the two buckets of water. From the corner of her eye, she saw the wind carry an ember up to the roof of the barn.

The *thatched* roof.

Oh, no! Every structure on Prudence's property had a roof made of straw and walls of wood, Phoebe realized—perfect materials for a mega-bonfire. If Phoebe didn't stop the fire now, everything Prudence owned could be gone in minutes!

Phoebe's heart hammered as she struggled with the heavy water buckets. If only she could freeze time like Piper until she doused this fire!

The wind wasn't helping. It seemed to be taking orders from the demon. With a whoosh it set the burning embers down on the edge of the barn's thatched roof. Phoebe's eyes widened with horror. "No!" she shouted, forcing her legs to run. But shouting at the fire was as effective as shouting at the demon.

The muscles in Phoebe's shoulders and biceps burned. Black smoke rose from the scorched grass, stinging her eyes and throat. Coughing, she blinked back tears. She could feel heat on her face and hands. Still, she forced herself closer to the barn.

"Aaaaa!" Phoebe jumped back as a spark caught close to her feet, only inches from the long skirt of the navy dress. Just then the door of the cottage flew open. Prudence and Hugh rushed outside, then froze in shock at the sight of the rapidly spreading fire.

"You did this?" Prudence shouted at Phoebe. Her face was taut with rage, and her eyes held a wicked gleam.

Phoebe shook her head furiously, but there was no time to explain.

"Stay away, you horrid girl!" Prudence shouted, snatching a bucket of water out of Phoebe's aching hands. "Stay away from my property!"

She emptied the bucket over a patch of grass burning close to the barn. Then, turning her back on Phoebe, she stormed over to grab some tools leaning against the barn. Hugh was already there, thrusting a pitchfork at the burning straw on the roof. Phoebe rushed over to help as he extracted a burning corner of the thatch and knocked it to the ground, clear of the building. Following Prudence's lead, Phoebe grabbed a shovel and helped beat out the flames.

As they worked, Phoebe noticed another

ember that had rolled against the barn, setting fire to the timber. She grabbed the second bucket of water and lugged it over. Then she realized that reaching the source of the fire meant she had to lean right into the flames.

Just do it quickly, she told herself. Scrunching her eyes shut against the smoke, she leaned over and emptied the heavy bucket. Beneath her the fire sizzled and smoked. For a second she felt the blazing heat on her skin, and smelled the fabric of her dress being singed. Then she was running from the fire, the empty bucket still in her hand.

"We need more water!" Prudence shouted.

Coughing and choking, Phoebe nodded. She raced for the creek, filled the bucket, and lugged it back. Then she did the same with the second bucket. She kept fetching water until the fire was under control.

Phoebe blinked. The crisis was over, and the barn was safe. Relieved, she turned to Prudence. The woman was shaking with rage.

"Have you gone mad?" Prudence demanded, kicking an empty bucket at Phoebe's feet. "I send you for water and you set the barn afire!"

"I did *not* start that fire," Phoebe shot back. "And I nearly scorched myself trying to put it out." She wished she didn't sound so angry, but by now her nerves were fried.

"I'm sure it was a mistake," Hugh said,

holding up his hands like a preacher. "Patience, dear Prudence. What can we expect of a woman with such a simple mind that she cannot even remember her own past?"

Phoebe wasn't sure if she was insulted or glad to be defended. On the other hand, she couldn't say much in her own defense. Unless she could be sure that Prudence was a witch, demon name-dropping was not a good idea in seventeenth-century Salem.

"A simple mind, indeed," Prudence said, leaning the shovel against the side of the barn. She pushed back a strand of blond hair that had become unpinned. Her blue eyes were icy cold as she glared at Phoebe. "One more *mistake*, and it will be *you* who is burning, Phoebe Halliwell."

Watching Prudence march back into the house, Phoebe sighed. Something was wrong with that woman. Bad mood or not, she was totally different from the kind, generous spirit who had nearly adopted Phoebe yesterday.

"You're welcome," Phoebe muttered under her breath, stamping on a glowing ember. She grabbed a rake and pushed some of the still glowing embers farther from the barn.

"Don't mind her," Hugh told her.

Phoebe was bending down over the rake when she felt him press against her. He slipped his arm around her waist, leaning over to whisper in her ear, "A lovely young thing such as you shouldn't be raking coals."

"Hello?" Phoebe squirmed, wriggling out of his grasp. "What do you think you're doing?" She couldn't believe he was coming on to her this way. And with Prudence barely out of sight!

Hugh's gray eyes were fixed on her body, making Phoebe want to squirm even more. Was this guy slime, or what?

"Playing hard to get?" he asked with a grin. "The game is part of the pleasure, isn't it? But you don't have to be coy with me. Do we not know each other well? My eyes will never forget the sight of you—every inch of your sweet, soft skin—in the middle of the village."

"Well, maybe it's time that you got a little temporary amnesia," Phoebe said, backing away. Her fingers closed over the rake, itching to lift it up and give Hugh a well-deserved whack on the head. Down, girl, she told herself. He's the least of your worries right now. Instead, she said, "You know, I'll bet Prudence is really upset right now. Why don't you go cheer her up? Make her some smelly root tea or something."

"An excellent idea," Hugh said, nodding slyly. "We must keep Prudence happy if we're going to be allowed to play our games."

The only game we're going to play is hide-and-seek, Phoebe thought. I'm going to hide, and you're not going to find me, you worm!

With a smoldering look, Hugh turned and headed into the cottage.

One problem down, another lurking in the shadows. Phoebe leaned on the rake and checked the horizon. Where would that demon pop up next? And just what was his plan?

Whatever the evil, there was one thing she knew for sure. She had to stop him. *Before* he found her again.

CHAPTER
7

Prue slapped a twenty-dollar bill into the palm of the delivery guy and slammed the heavy front door in his face. She had no patience for niceties like hello and goodbye.

She hurried into the kitchen, ready to devour the food. It seemed that lately she was hungry all the time. Maybe it had to do with the empty feeling she'd had inside ever since Phoebe had disappeared a few days ago. Too bad the smell wafting from the bags wasn't the greatest.

"What did you order?" she snapped at Piper, who sat at the kitchen table, flipping through a food magazine.

"I told you I was getting Chinese," Piper answered.

"And I told *you* I wasn't in the mood for Chinese." Prue slammed the bags onto the table and folded her arms.

"No," Piper argued. "You said you didn't want sweet and sour. This is hot and sour. There is a difference."

"Whatever," Prue said. She yanked at the kitchen drawer—too hard. It flew out and onto the floor. Silverware clattered onto the tiles.

"I told you that drawer was broken," Piper said.

"And I told *you* to get it fixed," Prue answered. She stepped over the drawer, kicked a pile of spoons aside, and sat at the table. Who needed silverware when chopsticks would work just fine? "Might as well dig in," she said, pulling a pair of chopsticks out of one bag.

"Aren't you going to clean that up?" Piper asked.

Opening a quart of steaming rice, Prue shrugged. "What's the point? The drawer is broken."

" 'The drawer is broken,' " Piper mimicked her. "Like that makes it all right to just leave it there?"

"Do you have to argue about everything?" Prue asked. She bit into a crunchy egg roll. The past few days had been a chain of petty arguments with Piper, and Prue was getting sick of it. Piper was just going to have to stop being a cranky little whiner. "What is wrong with you anyway?" she demanded.

"Nothing!" Piper insisted, jabbing a piece of kung pao chicken. She nibbled the food, then slammed down her chopsticks. "What am I saying? The answer is *everything*. Everything is wrong, okay?"

Prue licked her fingers. Piper could be so melodramatic. "Well, that's nothing new. Things just never go right for poor, poor Piper, do they?"

"Oh, come on, Prue. You know that we've been snapping at each other ever since Phoebe disappeared."

"True," Prue agreed. Not that it was her fault. But who was supposed to pick up the pieces and put everything back together again? Time and again, the great problem-solver of the Halliwell sisters was Prue. Well, she was getting sick of doing all the work.

"You know," Piper began, "this whole mess started with you. You're the one who just had to have a new pair of boots. You couldn't have waited another day, could you? If you had, none of this would ever have happened!"

"Me?" Prue wanted to toss the cold sesame noodles right down Piper's shirt. "Oh, sure. So it's my fault you couldn't stand your ground when that warlock tossed that wooden crate at you?"

"I was okay!" Piper insisted. "You could have gone after Phoebe."

Prue glared at her sister. "Don't even *think*

about blaming me, Piper, because I'm not going to be held responsible for this one, okay?" She pushed away from the table and crossed to the counter, silverware scattering as she walked.

"What's happening to you?" Piper's voice trembled. "When did you get so harsh?"

Oh, please! Prue thought. If Piper broke down in tears one more time, she was going to scream. It wasn't easy living with Ms. Sensitivity. Lately all Piper seemed able to do was moan and groan about poor Phoebe. Not that Prue wasn't worried about her. She was. But while Piper licked her wounds, Prue was more inclined to grab a sword and charge ahead.

"This is so awful," Piper moaned. "I can't think straight at work. I can barely *get* to work. The club is just a lot of loud noise and blurred faces. All I can think about is Phoebe and how we left her out there . . . somewhere." She pushed a carton of food away and put her head on the table. "I can't live this way."

Prue felt her anger begin to fade. She couldn't bear to see Piper look so broken. She set her food down on the counter. "Listen," she said more gently, "we're going to get Phoebe back. There's got to be something else we can do."

Piper sighed. "We've searched *The Book of Shadows* every day and every night. I just don't think there's a spell to find someone stuck under a warlock's spell."

"I'd love to get my hands on that warlock," Prue said, her anger returning. She went to the table and picked up another egg roll. She pointed it at Piper. "And you give up too easily. You always have. We need to keep looking in the book."

Piper lifted her head. "Right. And there you go, bossing me around again. Can't you ever just back off?"

Prue dipped the egg roll in some duck sauce and turned away. "Nope," she said flatly. "Come on. Let's get to the attic."

She climbed the stairs, hearing Piper's footsteps dragging behind her. That girl could slip into a funk faster than Prue could blink. Well, Piper could just as easily be depressed sitting in the attic as in the kitchen.

Up in the attic, Prue was still chewing her egg roll when she opened *The Book of Shadows*. Oops, a greasy fingerprint appeared on one of the pages. Usually things like that bothered her, but not anymore. After all, a girl had to eat. She wiped her hands on her jeans and kept leafing through the pages.

Piper sank into a chair beside an old typewriter and frowned. "It's hopeless."

Prue glared at her sister, then turned back to the book.

She came to a spell for taming beasts.

Something about the spell seemed odd. Prue blinked at the words. They seemed to swim before her eyes. "It can't be," she murmured.

"What can't?" Piper asked listlessly.

"This spell. It's changing," Prue said. She watched as the letters stretched and shrank and rearranged themselves into a new group of words.

"Changing? How?"

Prue stared at the book. "When I opened to this page, the spell was called 'For Taming Beasts.' But now it reads, 'For Maiming Beasts.'"

"You've overtired," Piper said.

"'Maiming beasts,'" Prue repeated. "Ha! That's sort of funny!"

"What is?"

"Nothing. Never mind." Prue waved her off. She didn't have time to explain the joke to Whiny Girl.

Her finger trailed down the page, stopping on the word warlock.

She held her breath as she read the spell. Yes! Yes!

"That's it!" Prue announced. She pointed to the spell. "Look, Piper! It's perfect!"

Phoebe sneezed at the dust and feathers that rose as she vigorously swept out the chicken coop. It was her gazillionth chore of the day and one of the dirtiest so far. Who knew that these little cluckers could be so foul, she thought. She shooed a few of the birds away so that she could finish.

All day long Prudence had been popping in and out of the cottage, sometimes telling Phoebe to rest, other times telling her, basically, to get her butt in gear. It was as if Prudence was a different person. First she was the kind, generous soul, then she was her evil twin, who'd be happy to see Phoebe slip into the stinky mud of the pigsty. It was enough to give Phoebe a whole new perspective on her ancestors.

Who knew insanity ran in the family? she thought.

With the chicken coop swept, she turned to shoo the chickens back inside. "Okay, girls, the dorm's clean now. Next time you want to trash the place, take it outside."

"What are you doing?" Prudence called from across the clearing. She had been weeding the garden with Cassandra, who now trailed her mother from a cautious distance. "Did I not tell you to chop the wood before you swept the chicken coop?" Prudence demanded, her hands on her hips.

Actually, you didn't, Phoebe wanted to say, but she bit her tongue. No use crossing Prudence's "evil twin" persona.

Instead, Phoebe just leaned the broom against the chicken coop and shook the dust out of her apron. "So, where's the woodpile?" she asked.

Prudence pointed her to the back of the cottage, then marched inside with Cassandra.

Phoebe glanced down at her hands. They were blistered and red. Her legs were tired, her throat was dry, and now she was off to chop wood. Well, at least she'd be getting in a solid aerobic workout.

Phoebe's eyes swept the surrounding forest before she headed over to the woodpile. Now that she knew the demon had it in for her, she had to be careful. Now that she knew he was near, she expected to find him lurking in every shadow.

Swallowing hard, Phoebe winced. Her throat was on fire. She needed a drink, which meant going into the cottage and risking Prudence's wrath. It was a chance she'd have to take.

Pushing open the door, Phoebe spied Cassandra curled up in the chair beside the fireplace for an afternoon nap. Now, *that* was a good idea.

A cup of root tea sat half-empty on the kitchen table.

Nearby, Prudence knelt at the side table—the one with the candles and the wooden bowl. The candles were lit, casting a warm circle of light over Prudence's golden hair. Leaning over a large book, her hair pouring over her shoulders, she was still and quiet, totally engrossed, drawing something in the book.

As the door closed behind her, Phoebe caught a look at the book. It was *The Book of Shadows,* and Prudence was adding to it!

Phoebe looked over Prudence's shoulder. She read the title of a spell she was writing: "For Maiming Beasts."

Maiming? That was weird. Phoebe didn't remember seeing any spells for maiming in *The Book of Shadows*. But really, who cared? The book was here. That meant Prudence definitely was a witch *and* an ancestor. Maybe they could work together to find a spell to banish the demon and another spell to send Phoebe home.

Relieved, Phoebe almost fell to the floor beside Prudence. "Blessed be," she said softly, using the traditional greeting shared by witches through the centuries.

Prudence flinched, then glanced up at Phoebe with a startled expression.

"What? Why did you say that?" she gasped.

"The book," Phoebe said, trying to hold back the huge smile that was bubbling inside her. "I see you're writing in *The Book of Shadows*. I know it's hard to believe, but I understand because—"

"I don't know what you're talking about!" Prudence slammed the book closed, clutching it against her chest. "This is . . . a family book— some recipes from my mother."

"It's all right, Prudence," Phoebe assured her. "I understand about spells and powers. I even—"

"There will be no talk of such evil in this house," Prudence snapped. Still clutching the book, she blew out the candles and plopped down in a chair at the main table. "This is a book of family recipes, nothing more."

Cold, crisp, final. The words hit Phoebe as hard as the cast-iron skillet on the fire. Why was it every time she gained an inch with Prudence, she got pummeled back a few yards?

Phoebe stood up and brushed off the skirt of her dress. She probably ought to just chill and finish wood chopping. No sense getting Prudence even more wound up. But now that Phoebe had seen the book, it was hard to walk away from it. It was so familiar, like a dear friend. She ached to touch it, to search for the spells that might help her. She wanted to rip that book right out of Prudence's hands. But that could backfire—badly.

No, it would be better to approach the book when Prudence wasn't around to protest. At least now Phoebe knew *The Book of Shadows* was here. And it was so close—just a few feet away.

Closing her eyes, Phoebe tried to visualize the information she was searching for. All she got were images of letters written in a flowing script and pages that were brown at the edges. Not enough to really get her anywhere.

"Begging your pardon," Prudence said curtly. "But don't you have a good amount of wood to chop?"

"Yes, right. I just came in for a drink." Phoebe shook herself back to the present. She poured herself some water from a pitcher and lifted the mug, never taking her eyes off Prudence.

You can play coy with me, sister, Phoebe thought, but now I've seen the book. I'll find it later, somewhere, somehow.

Maybe, just maybe, there would be a spell inside for banishing the demon and sending Phoebe home.

All she had to do was get her hands on it.

CHAPTER

8

A spell for summoning warlocks!" Prue exclaimed. "I can't believe I didn't notice it before."

Piper got up, glanced at the page, and shrugged. "Who cares?" She stretched out on a throw rug on the floor and studied the ceiling.

Ignoring her, Prue read on. "Hmm," she muttered. "If you're searching for a particular warlock, the spell has to be cast 'where the warlock last was manifest.' "

Piper shuddered. "Somehow I don't think revisiting that alley is the best idea."

Prue frowned. Let's see what else the spell calls for." She read the list of ingredients, which ran down the page. It included everything from rose thorns to nail clippings to white candles. Luckily, there was nothing too exotic that would take days to track down.

On the opposite page was an illustration of a monstrous man doubled over. The title of the page was "Potions and Spells for the Warding Off and Ruination of Warlocks."

"Ooh! It gives a list of nasty ways to get rid of warlocks, too," Prue reported. "I wish we'd had this before."

"Hello? Prue, what does this have to do with Phoebe?" Piper asked.

Lifting *The Book of Shadows* from its stand, Prue clutched it against her chest and carried it over to Piper. She sat on the attic floor with the fat book in her lap. "A warlock did *something* to Phoebe. Whether he cast a spell on her or sent her to Tahiti, that yellow-eyed warlock had something to do with our sister's disappearance."

"Duh!" Piper glared at her. "Tell me something I don't already know."

"Well, if a warlock was the key to Phoebe's disappearance, don't you think it would be a good idea to seek that warlock out?" Prue's fingernails tapped the open page in *The Book of Shadows*. "This is like a tracking spell."

"Great," Piper said. "So we find the warlock pond scum who made Phoebe disappear. Then what? We ask him to please undo his spell?"

Prue took a deep calming breath. "No," she explained patiently. "We find the warlock pond scum and we *force* him to tell us how to get her back. Right here: the 'ruination' of said warlock. I think it's going to give us major ammo. Either he brings Phoebe back or he dies."

The flash of intelligence in Piper's brown eyes told Prue that she got it. Something had clicked—finally.

"How soon can we start?" Piper asked.

Prue smiled. "How many rose thorns do you think we'll need to make up a quarter cup?"

"Someone's coming!" Prue whispered. She and Piper had managed to pull the spell together in an hour, and here they were, not far from where they'd lost Phoebe, watching as the bait approached the hook.

Piper peered down at the man below. Prue followed her gaze, squinting. He was just starting to climb the steep stairs cut into one of San Francisco's nearly vertical hillsides. The stairway led to the North Beach alley. He looked like an ordinary guy, but the fine hairs on the back of Prue's neck were standing straight up. It was as if a neon sign were flashing in every cell of her body: Warning! Warlock approaching!

"Careful, we don't want to scare him off," Piper said.

A cool breeze was blowing through, along

with wispy white clouds that shrouded whole sections of the Bay Bridge before they danced off into the sky. Prue took a deep breath. Although she didn't want to admit it to Piper, there was no denying the anticipation she was feeling. Something was going to happen tonight.

They were going to get Phoebe back.

Prue kept her eyes on the stairway. By the single light shining above it, she couldn't make out the man's face, but she could see that he wore a black shirt and trench coat. He was a couple of steps up the steep flight of stairs when he stopped, glanced around quickly, then made a sign in the air with his left hand and vanished.

A second later he reappeared about a third of the way from the top. "That's it. He blinked." Prue squeezed Piper's arm. "He's a warlock."

Prue could feel a change in her sister. Piper's body was suddenly taut with tension. Maybe that meant she was ready for a battle.

"Oh, you are going to be so helpful," Prue spoke quietly to the warlock as he headed toward them. "You're just what we ordered. I can't believe the spell worked."

"Well, it did," Piper agreed, ducking back into the shadow of a doorway. "And he's right on time." She leaned against the marble wall, her dark eyes frightened. "Are you sure about this, Prue?" she asked. "I mean, we've never actually gone out and *hunted* warlocks before. We usually wait until the slime-molds come after us, the way that one did with Phoebe."

Glancing down the stairs, Prue saw that the warlock was slowly climbing again, and he wasn't far from the top. This was no time for cold feet. She ducked into Piper's doorway and spoke in a whisper, "What, exactly, is your point?"

"It just seems so . . . so cold-blooded," Piper answered. "We promised to use our powers to do good. Remember? Harm no one. Now we're waiting to snag someone who maybe hasn't done anything to hurt anyone we know."

"What?"

"What if we've got the wrong warlock? That spell wasn't real specific."

"He's a warlock, Piper." Prue's words were raspy in the cold air. "Warlock equals evil. And we're taking things one step at a time. It's the only way to track Phoebe."

Piper stared in the direction of the approaching figure. "Umm, Prue? That's not the warlock who took Phoebe." She pointed at the man.

Prue squinted. Now that he was closer, he did look different from the creepoid she remembered. But so what? "You know warlocks," she argued. "They hang around together. Like a club. This guy could know our guy. He could know about Phoebe."

The scuffing sound of footsteps on the stairs ended all discussion. The warlock was one step away from them. It was now or never.

Peering out from the doorway, Prue saw his shadow ascend to the top step, then round the landing. Excitement coursed through her veins as she stepped out of the doorway, startling him. He paused, staring at Prue with confusion in his eyes.

Piper emerged a second later, her face holding an expression of sheer determination.

Glancing at the two sisters, the warlock seemed to get it—way too quickly. Rearing back, he started to raise his hands, ready to attack. No way, Prue thought. He was not going to hurt one of them before they had a chance to question him.

"Freeze him!" Prue ordered.

With a flick of her hand, Piper used her power to suspend time. The warlock became perfectly still, his magic stopped before it even started.

Relieved, Prue crossed the landing, her boots clicking on the cement. "Hello, hello." He was an average-looking guy, taller than most, with thick, silver hair and deep blue eyes. Not a bad catch, if he weren't obsessed with harnessing the power of evil.

She glared into his eyes. This guy was going

to pay. He was going to pay for what his friend had done to Phoebe.

Piper rushed over beside her, then paused nervously a few feet from the warlock. "Okay, so here we are." She gestured toward the frozen figure. "Any ideas on what we're going to do now?"

Definitely, Prue thought. Somehow, she knew exactly what to do. It was almost like an instinct.

She stepped right up to the man, face-to-face, and placed her hands flat on his chest. Her hands began to glow in the darkness.

Her fingers and palms became red-orange, neon-bright against his black shirt. The sight was mesmerizing.

"Prue!" Piper screamed. "Your hands! What's happening?"

Prue wasn't sure. But the sensation surging through her hands was so incredible, she couldn't possibly break the connection.

What was that? A flutter of movement? Piper's time freeze was ending. At once the warlock began to writhe and scream. His face contorted in pain, and his eyes bulged from his head in horror.

But Prue did not let go.

A white, ashen paste covered the warlock's skin. His face wrinkled. His broad shoulders and chest caved in. Was he shrinking? The tall man seemed to be drying up and shriveling like a raisin. Prue winced as her hands fell into a mushy area of his chest, but she didn't back off. She couldn't back away from the awesome feeling her touch was generating.

"Aarrrggg!" the warlock's voice bubbled up, pleading and pathetic.

"What is going on?" Piper demanded again. "Prue! I thought we were going to ask him about Phoebe!"

Prue didn't answer. She couldn't. Words were secondary to the gigantic thing that was happening here. An electrifying sensation was passing through her, and she needed every ounce of concentration to soak it up completely.

The warlock's entire body was now made of white ash. Prue watched in amazement as he collapsed in on himself, then turned to powder.

Stunned, Prue dropped to her knees in the pile of white dust.

"Prue!" Piper called. Her voice was laced with fear. "Are you okay?"

Huddled on the ground, Prue felt her sister's arms slip around her, offering emotional and physical support. "Come on, I'll help you up," Piper whispered gently.

But Prue tore away, leaping to her feet. "Wow! I'm fine! I don't need help at all." The truth was, she was more than fine. She felt magnificent!

Rubbing her hands over the sleeves of her jacket, Prue detected something different, something new inside her. A total energy blast coursing through her, making her feel stronger than ever. "Well, that was a large charge." She chuckled.

"What?" Piper asked. "Prue, tell me what happened."

Prue gritted her teeth. Couldn't Piper figure out anything for herself? She was going to have to tone it down a notch or her annoyance factor was going to put Prue over the edge.

"What do you think happened, Piper?" she said, trying not to snarl at her sister. "He's gone and we're here. And before he left, something passed from him to me. Something huge." Her voice dropped. "It felt like his powers went straight into me. It was phenomenal."

"Get out!" Piper's mouth dropped open in awe. "You're telling me you soaked up a warlock's powers? Is that even possible? I mean . . . whoa."

Prue closed her eyes, letting herself take a deep breath. She felt great. The air smelled so clean and promising. This wasn't what she'd expected from tonight, but she certainly wasn't complaining. She glanced over at her sister. "It's like I'm running on new juice, Piper. Think about it: new powers."

Piper seemed confused as she tugged on one of the snaps on her jacket. "Okay, truth-

fully? When I think about it, absorbing warlock juice could be a little dicey."

"And I'm telling you I've never felt better."

"Still," Piper said, "we ought to get you
home to sort out what happened."

"Home?" Feeling a surge of power, Prue
closed her eyes again and laughed.

"What's so funny?"

"My new powers," Prue said, reaching out.
She took Piper's hand and squeezed.

A tingling sensation shot through Prue. Yes!
Her new powers were working.

Before Prue's eyes, Piper's body went
totally flat and two-dimensional, like a bill-
board. Considering the odd sensations she was
experiencing, Prue assumed the same was
happening to herself.

Piper's postcard body folded into itself,
until it was folded into a piece so tiny it
seemed to disappear.

Prue could feel her body doing the same
thing. Bye-bye alley, she thought.

Prue could feel that she was suddenly in a
different place. The air was warmer, the lights
were softer. There was a familiar scent of spicy
potpourri. When Prue could see again, she
realized she was standing in the parlor of
Halliwell Manor.

Across the room, right beside Gram's velvet
Queen Anne chair, Piper was unfolding. The
small square doubled, then opened again and

again until Piper stood there, flat and motion-
less on the Chinese rug.

With a whoosh, Piper's image rounded out,
and she was the moving, breathing, three-
dimensional Piper again. Of course, she was
also the annoying, cautious, solemn Piper
again.

Prue's mind reeled. They'd been trans-
ported home in a millisecond. This would
make for one easy commute to Buckland's—if
she still had a job there. She'd missed a few
days of work with no explanation. Prue
wanted to laugh. Maybe they'd fire her!

Piper tugged on a sleeve that had ridden up
as she unfolded. "I feel like I was made into a
paper doll. Did you have to flatten me?"

Prue shrugged. "I don't know," she admitted. "I'm not used to this power yet." But she
couldn't pretend to be all worried about it.
Like *some* people. In fact, she was so far from
worried, she could barely keep a straight face.
She threw her head back and let out a long, full
laugh.

Excellent! What a rush!

Phoebe straightened up in the center of the
field and swatted at a fat black fly. "Dive-bomb
me one more time and I'll squash you," she
muttered through clenched teeth.

It was the next day, and farm life was sinking lower and lower on her list of fun things to

try in the new millennium. At least she'd given it an earnest effort this morning. Today she'd hauled water and split wood before she got near a crumb of breakfast. She'd even agreed to tie on Prudence's ugly old bonnet and work in the fields. Now she looked like that old maid in the butter commercial.

She heard the barn door swing open. "Phoebe!"

Phoebe winced. The sound was like fingernails on a blackboard. When Prudence's voice hit that sharp, nasty tone Phoebe could feel her entire body recoil. Prudence was definitely going with the "evil twin" persona today.

"I fail to see how you can weed the garden when you're standing upright," Prudence said.

Phoebe turned to face her and saw Cassandra at Prudence's side. "I was just stretching out my back." She smiled brightly and demonstrated a couple of windmill toe touches from aerobics class. "And one and two and three—"

Cassandra laughed, but Prudence's mouth straightened into a tight little frown. "Never have I met anyone with so many shameful excuses!"

Okay! All right already! Phoebe gave in. If she was going to make any progress finding the demon and researching a spell, she needed to get Prudence off her case. She squatted down again and yanked out a handful of bristly weeds. Her crimson nail polish glimmered in the sun. It was amazing how her manicure had held up, considering the chores Prudence had assigned her so far. Wow, what brand of polish had she used?

Maybe that wasn't the most pressing question. What she really needed to know was how to get Prudence to own up to the family talent. Phoebe blew a strand of brown hair out of her face.

A pounding sound rose in the distance—the steady gallop of a horse.

Phoebe stood up to watch the horse and carriage clatter down the road from the village. Hugh was waving excitedly from the driver's seat.

Old Gray Eyes. After the way he'd come on to her yesterday, he wasn't exactly a welcome sight. On the other hand, any excuse to pluck a few less weeds was welcome.

"Prudence!" he called, reining in the horse. "Come quickly! You are needed in the village."

"What is it, Hugh?" Prudence asked.

"Mrs. Gibbs is in need of a midwife. The baby is coming."

"But it can't be." Prudence's hands flew to her face. "The child is weeks early!" She picked up her basket and ran toward the cottage. "Come along, Cassandra. I'll fetch the medicine bag. Take off your apron, child. Run!"

The little girl darted across the field and followed her mother into the cottage.

"And good morning to you, Phoebe," Hugh said with a big smile.

"Whatever." Hitching up her skirt to keep it from dragging in the field, Phoebe bent down once again. Her fingers closed over a wiry clump of weeds. Wait a minute, she thought. With everyone out of the house and off in the village for a while, this will be the perfect chance for me to find *The Book of Shadows*. She wasn't exactly sure what she should look for inside it, but she knew that she needed help—big time. Since yesterday's face-off with the demon, she'd been feeling pretty helpless. Okay, very helpless. She was stuck playing Cinderella while he was out conjuring up a big evil stew.

Phoebe blinked. Somehow, she found herself weeding around a big pair of black boots. She looked up. Hugh towered over her like a jolly giant.

"Are the thistles so fascinating?" he asked, bending down beside her.

Phoebe bit her lip. She hated the way he checked her out, his eyes roving over her constantly. And she'd thought he was a hero? Boy, was that a mistake.

"Have you lost your tongue?" He picked a weed and dangled the end over her, tickling her neck.

Phoebe swiped at it and missed. "My tongue is fine, thanks. And stop that! Have you lost your mind?"

Hugh laughed as he dipped the weed lower, aiming at her cleavage.

"I said, cut it out!" She ripped the weed out of his hand. "That's it, pal. I've had enough of your slimy looks and suggestive remarks. As far as I'm concerned, you have a relationship with that woman in there." She pointed toward the cottage. "Not with me. You have nothing with me."

From the expression on his face she couldn't tell if he was surprised or amused. "I do believe you're wrong, Phoebe." He reached out to her outstretched arm, grabbed her hand, then planted a kiss on her knuckles.

"Oh, gross." She winced, wiping her hand against her dress. "Read my lips: I don't want your cooties, Hugh."

Again he laughed. "Cooties? Truly, you say the most remarkable—"

"We are ready to go," called a voice.

Phoebe and Hugh swung toward the cottage to see Prudence standing a few feet in front of the door. Medicine bag in hand, she stood as stiff and cold as a statue. Something dark and sad glimmered in her light blue eyes: suspicion. It was clear that she'd seen the kiss, and she wasn't too happy about it.

Snapping back to his polite persona, Hugh strapped Prudence's bag onto the carriage and helped her into the seat. The cottage door slammed and Cassandra raced out. She joined them inside the carriage.

Phoebe sank back into the field and yanked out a particularly stubborn clump of weeds. As she watched the carriage leave, she held her breath. She had to be patient just a few moments longer. She waited until the clip-clop of the horse's hooves faded away.

Finally! Phoebe darted into the cottage and began looking for the book. It wasn't in any of the obvious places—on the pine table, by the altar, or on Prudence's nightstand. Maybe the book wasn't in the cottage at all. What if Prudence kept it in the barn or something?

No. Phoebe shook her head. She was fairly certain that no witch would keep *The Book of Shadows* too far from reach. Still, it was definitely not in sight. Okay, so she'd have to do a little detective work.

Phoebe searched every cupboard. She emptied trunks. She peered under the mattresses. She even started feeling for loose floorboards. With a flash of inspiration she checked the hearth, wondering if the book could be hidden under a skillet or something. Not a very bright idea, but then again, Prudence was more than a little weird.

When the fireplace turned out to be a dead end, Phoebe spun around. She stood there biting a fingernail. "I know you're here. Where are you?" she called to the book she loved so much.

She noticed a chair that Prudence kept moving around the cottage. Could the thick volume be hidden under there?

No, there was no place to hide anything under the wood seat—but wait. Phoebe lifted her gaze to stare up at the thatched ceiling. Had Prudence been moving the chair to get to something up there? Phoebe climbed onto the chair and reached up.

Bingo!

There, tucked between the exposed beam and some straw thatching, was *The Book of Shadows*.

She slid it out and jumped off the chair with the book cradled in her arms. Usually, the book gave her a warm, comforting feeling when she touched it. Today, though, it made her shiver. What was that about? She went to the table and cracked it open.

Sitting there, Phoebe smoothed back the pages of the book she knew so well. She nearly gasped when she saw all the empty space inside. Then she quickly realized that Prudence was only the second generation of witches to write in *The Book of Shadows*. By the time Gram had passed the book on to Phoebe and her sisters, many women had contributed to the drawings and information inscribed between the covers. Since she was more than three hundred years into the past, most of that work just hadn't been done yet.

Which means that there aren't that many spells here, Phoebe thought. Oh, please have the ones I need!

Flipping to the end, Phoebe saw pages and pages that were empty. She ran one hand over the blank parchment and—wham! A vision filled her mind.

It was of a strange, skewed world—a dark, shadowed place. Through the dust and shadows she saw Prue and Piper, but their faces were painted with dark lines, and they were wearing lots of leather and chains. Prue and Piper as biker chicks at a costume party? Not exactly their style.

They were hunched down beside something on a dark, deserted road. What were they doing? Hiding? Waiting for some secret rendezvous? Phoebe wasn't sure.

Then she recognized a dangerous glimmer in Prue's eye, the kind she got when she was fighting warlocks.

The vision wavered then became clear again. Something was moving farther down the road—someone was coming toward them—and Prue and Piper were on their feet, looking different somehow. They reminded Phoebe of the way Kit, the family cat, looked before she sprang to attack.

Prue focused her powers on the guy on the road, and a scream of agony rang out. "Score!" Prue said.

"The next one is mine," Piper told her.

A shiver ran through Phoebe as the vision faded. What was that about? Whatever it was, it looked completely ugly.

Were her sisters hunting warlocks? It didn't compute. Prue and Piper weren't the predatory type. Besides, that was totally against the oath they'd all taken when they discovered the Power of Three. What were her sisters thinking?

Yesterday's encounter with the demon flashed into her mind. He had threatened to turn her family members evil. Phoebe shuddered. Could his magic be working in the future already?

Now it's even more important to get rid of this demon and get home, Prue thought. Back to the book.

"How about a time-travel spell?" she asked aloud. It would be handy to have it ready. As soon as she took care of the demon, she was out of here. She flipped through the book without success.

"Not even close," she muttered as her eyes skimmed over a spell to make a dry cow give milk.

As she turned the pages she wondered when Prudence would be back. Really, it could be anytime. There was no telling how long Mrs. What's-her-name was going to take having that baby.

A hand-drawn illustration of a man with spikes shooting out of his head caught her eye. Under it was written, "Spell for Banishing the Most Evil of Demons."

Phoebe's mouth dropped open. This was it. "Yes!" she shouted, thrusting a fist in the air. Now all she needed was to collect the ingredients, find the demon, and bust his ugly face back to Hades.

She could start in on the ingredients right away, though she couldn't copy the list. Colonials didn't exactly keep extra pens and notepads handy. Her finger ran down the page. The spell called for simple ingredients—everything from dirt to spices.

There was just one minor glitch. The spell required the power of two or more witches. Phoebe was just one woman. How could she . . .

Wait a minute—what about Prudence? Somehow Phoebe needed to get Prudence to help her. Phoebe frowned. Not a likely scenario. How could she even ask when the woman's personality flip-flopped every hour? Getting Prudence involved seemed like a bad idea all around.

So who was going to help Phoebe with the spell?

I'll cross that bridge when I come to it, Phoebe thought.

She closed her eyes and repeated the ingredients she needed, trying to memorize them. " 'Soil from the earth where three roads meet, pinch of salt, needle of pine . . .' "

With the list fixed in her mind, Phoebe

leafed through the rest of the book, hoping for a spell to get her out of Salem, but there simply weren't that many spells in this version of *The Book of Shadows*. She found herself flipping to the end, to the entries Prudence had made in the past few days. She paused a moment to look at an illustration. It was of a deer, with bleeding lacerations across its body.

"What the . . ." Phoebe cringed at the shocking sketch. Beside it was a curse to cast on enemies.

> Make an image of thy foe,
> Slash it as I slashed the roe.
> Then bury it beneath full moon
> In the grave of one hanged too soon.

Yuck! That is one evil spell, Phoebe thought with a shudder.

She turned another page and found a spell "To Be Revenged on One Who Has Done You Harm." A third spell was designed "To Cause Disease in One Who Crosses You."

Phoebe stared at the book openmouthed. These spells—she didn't remember ever seeing them in *The Book of Shadows* in the future. So how could they be here now?

Phoebe was still leafing through the book when the door flew open.

Prudence stood in the doorway, her eyes fixed on Phoebe.

"Hey! You're back early," Phoebe said with forced cheerfulness. She wanted to slam *The Book of Shadows* closed and hide it behind her back, but it was too late. Prudence had caught her. And—big surprise—she didn't look too happy about it.

"What do you think you're doing?" Prudence's voice was soft but completely unnerving.

"Just checking something in your book," Phoebe answered, closing it gently and patting the cover.

Prudence marched across the room, lunging for her.

"But don't worry," Phoebe rattled on, darting out of the way. "I'll finish the weeding. And I didn't forget about the chickens or the—"

Prudence grabbed the collar of Phoebe's dress so tightly that Phoebe could feel her fingernails digging into her neck.

"I—you're going to rip it," Phoebe screeched. But Prudence kept pulling. Nose to nose with her ancestor, Phoebe couldn't miss the madness in the woman's eyes.

The tight collar constricted her throat, but Phoebe forced herself to hang tough. She stared into the face of evil as Prudence scowled at her.

"If I ever, *ever*, catch you touching this book again," Prudence said in a clear, calm voice, "I will kill you."

CHAPTER 9

The bleep of a ringing phone pierced the halls of Halliwell Manor.

Upstairs in her room, Piper leaned into the mirror and added another layer of eyeliner around her eyes. "Can you get that?" she shouted to Prue.

The phone kept ringing, and Piper cursed her older sister for being so slow to answer.

Tilting her head to the side, Piper leaned in again and drew another line of black over her eyes. She'd always been so careful, so conservative with makeup, but for some reason, in the past few days she felt wild and willing to experiment. Layering was so cool, and black on black was such a great look.

"Well," she said aloud, talking to her reflection, "if you're going to the dark side, you might as well look the part." She slid open a tube of lip gloss and applied a silvery white sheen to her lips.

Now I look dead, she thought. Perfect for a night of destruction.

Tonight's plan was nothing new. Piper and Prue were going to do the spell for seeking out warlocks. Been there, done that. The big, beautiful difference was that this time Piper would be the one to suck up the warlock's powers. Yum-yum.

It was a good thing, because she was really, really hungry.

Piper collapsed back on her bed with a satisfied laugh. Cravings for power—that was a first. Then again, there'd been a few firsts in the five days since Phoebe had disappeared. Was it just last Saturday that it had happened? And what was today . . . Thursday? Or Friday?

The phone was ringing again.

"Prue!" Piper yelled. "Are you going to get that or what?"

"I'm busy!" Prue called from her room.

"Doing what?" Piper pushed herself up and headed down the hall. She couldn't imagine what could be occupying her sister's time.

Neither of them had gotten around to cleaning the house this week. She paused in Prue's doorway and frowned. "What are you doing to yourself?"

"Tattoos," Prue said, showing off a temporary tattoo of a thorny demon on her biceps. "Want one?"

"Maybe later. We've got to get going, or the spell is going to kick in before we get there."

"Picky, picky," Prue murmured, pressing another tattoo to her ankle.

The phone started ringing again. "I'll get it," Piper said, heading toward the staircase.

By the time she reached the kitchen, the ringing had stopped, but there were messages on the machine. She pushed the Play button. "Piper, it's Jason from the club," said a voice. Strains of music and laughter were in the background. "The bartender called in sick, and we've been waiting for you—"

Click. Piper cut him off. Okay, she hadn't been to the club for a few days, but what was the problem? People just needed to do their jobs and shut up. Maybe the old Piper would have freaked about missing work, but now she had more important things to do.

She played the other two messages on the machine. They were both for Prue, both from the auction house. It sounded as though Prue hadn't made it to work much this week, either. In one message her boss was acting all worried and sad that Prue was so sick. Ha! Sick with power was more like it.

Cutting off the message, Piper paused. What was that smell?

She turned toward the sink, obviously the source of the odor. Pots and dishes and glasses were piled high, some floating in a pool of scummy water. The floor was still scattered with silverware, which Prue had never had a chance to pick up. The place was a mess, but that wasn't Piper's problem.

Turning away from the smell, she went into the living room and paused. Piles of mail, catalogs, and papers covered the coffee table. Prue's unwashed laundry was heaped on the couch. And were those cobwebs on Gram's chandelier? The old thing was looking pretty dingy.

What a dump.

The old house had changed. Actually, a lot of things had changed, Piper reflected: The house. Her job. Her sister. It bothered Piper a little that everything in her life was sort of rotting away, but it wasn't her fault. It was all because of Phoebe. Phoebe had disappeared, and Piper's life was beginning to stink like this musty old house.

Passing by the foot of the stairs, Piper picked up a new odor. "Prue!" she yelled up the stairs. "Did you light a candle?"

Prue appeared at the top of the stairs, holding a tattoo patch over her wrist. "I'm always lighting candles. Ever since the electricity went out in that storm two nights ago."

"Because *you* forgot to call the electric company to get it fixed," Piper reminded her.

"I had a few things on my mind, okay? And what's your problem that you can't pick up a phone?"

Let's not get into another shouting match, Piper thought wearily. "Well, it smells like something is burning."

Prue's pert nose wrinkled as she sniffed the air. "Yes." She glanced behind her, nodding. "The attic. We lit those candles for the warlock-seeking spell. Didn't you blow them out?"

"I thought *you* were going to take care of it," Piper said as she raced up the stairs.

"And why would you think that?" Prue called after her. "Oh, I know. Because you weren't thinking!"

Piper was angry and breathless when she bounded into the smoky attic. Most of the candles had burned down and extinguished themselves. One of them had spilled wax all over a table, igniting an old doily. Now a crispy circle of lace, it was slowly smoldering.

It's a good thing *one* of us noticed, Piper thought, before we burned down the house. She grabbed the pitcher of spring water they'd used in the spell, doused the smoldering ash, then laughed. Somewhere in her logical mind she knew that it would be a horrible thing to lose their home, but another part of her just wanted to laugh, laugh as if none of it mattered.

She went over to *The Book of Shadows* and

pressed her hands against the open pages. The book made her shiver.

She pulled her hands away, staring at the spell written out on the page. It was a dark spell, a curse for someone who crosses you. On the opposite page was a drawing of a deer, cut all over its body and bleeding. Piper shuddered. Lately lots of spells like this had been appearing in the book. Piper didn't understand why, and Prue didn't seem to care. Actually, Prue seemed to enjoy them.

But then, Prue had been on a nasty tear ever since she'd sucked away that warlock's powers. Entirely full of herself. Totally annoying. It wasn't fair of her to take his powers for herself, but tonight that would change. It was Piper's turn to even the score.

They'd already cast the spell to attract another warlock. Now they just had to get into place so that everything could happen the way Piper had planned it.

She ducked out the attic door and raced down the stairs, shouting, "Prue! Get your butt downstairs. It's time to bag another warlock."

Piper's mouth was watering as she peered out of the shadows. Had she even eaten dinner? Lunch? She didn't remember, and it didn't really matter. It wasn't food she craved. It was something stronger: power.

A cold wind from the nearby water swept

through the empty alleys in this warehouse district. Piper and Prue were hiding in the shadows beside an abandoned warehouse, just a few yards from a ghostly quiet street. They were about twenty yards away from a biker bar, which was a key part of their plan.

The buzz of an engine caught Piper's attention. She nudged her sister and watched the empty street. Soon a single headlight appeared in the distance.

Only it wasn't a normal white motorcycle headlight. Rings of colored light pulsed and glowed around it.

"Warlock on a Harley," Piper whispered. "And he's going to be mine."

The biker passed under a streetlight, and Piper saw the long, curved metal fenders of a classic Harley-Davidson motorcycle. This time there was no fear or hesitation clouding Piper's mind. This time the hunt was exciting.

"Ready?" she asked Prue, who nodded.

Just as the biker approached the alley where they were hiding, Piper used her powers to freeze time.

The Harley stood suspended in the center of the street.

"Nice balance," Piper taunted the frozen warlock.

Prue picked up an old railroad tie on the side of the road and slid it directly into the biker's path.

Time restored and the motorcycle buzzed ahead. Within seconds the bike hit the huge piece of wood. The Harley and its driver flew into the air, out of control. The warlock landed on his side, a few feet from the twisted wreckage of the bike.

Piper and Prue rushed over to his body. Kneeling beside him, Piper thrust her hands onto his chest, frantic to get his powers.

"Why?" The word scraped out of his throat. His sad eyes were slightly open.

Piper felt creeped out by his question. Shouldn't he be dead already?

"You're a warlock, that's why," Prue explained to the man coldly. "And last I heard, warlocks are evil."

This is for Phoebe, Piper wanted to say. She knew it was all *because* of Phoebe, though she wasn't quite sure how it all connected together anymore.

The warlock closed his eyes and collapsed onto the pavement as Piper felt a cold, thrilling chill travel up her arms.

Piper felt the warlock's body disintegrating beneath her hands. His bones were softening, dissolving. For a split second he stiffened and shook beneath her hands. Then his body imploded—turned to dust—and the remainder of his powers shot straight into Piper.

"Whoooo!" Piper let out a squeal. Her head reeled. Suddenly she felt lighter, stronger, as though she could run a marathon without even breathing hard. She was revved, charged. Energy was streaming through her. She'd never felt so wildly alive. This was it! This was the surge that had lit up Prue's life.

With a quiet smile, Piper watched the wind carry away the dust that had once been the warlock's body. She closed her eyes and laughed. Power theft! If it was so evil, why did it feel so good?

CHAPTER
10

Phoebe walked slowly and cautiously through the village of Salem, Massachusetts. Prudence had sent her here to trade butter for spices, which she'd already taken care of. Even that simple task wasn't easy. Phoebe had to constantly remind herself to keep her head down, her eyes averted beneath her bonnet, her hands tucked inside the cloak Prudence had loaned her. People were watching her like a hawk, probably waiting for her to fling off her clothes and dance naked down the street.

Phoebe would have loved to treat them to a joke or two, but she had to behave. The last thing she needed was more trouble, especially now that she'd come so close to gathering a crucial ingredient for her demon-banishing spell.

"Soil from the earth where three roads meet" was what *The Book of Shadows* had specified. In a place and time where few roads existed, Phoebe knew the best spot to find a true intersection was in the village itself.

She passed two men leading horses and dared to lift her chin to stare ahead. At the other end of the lane was a fork in the road, just beyond the blacksmith's barn. Was that the three roads?

Strolling ahead, she patted the sacks of spices in her pockets. Most of them were for Prudence. One was for her spell. She was getting closer to having everything she needed. She'd already collected some of the easy stuff, like a thimble, a tea leaf, and two flat stones. Now she would have the soil.

Phoebe reached the intersection where three dirt roads crossed each other. Works for me, she thought. Hoping that no one would notice, she stooped behind a barrel and scooped some dirt into a leather pouch she'd swiped from Prudence's herb collection. Still squatting, she was just tying it up when she heard footsteps.

"Do you need help over there?" called a man.

Tilting her head around the barrel, Phoebe spotted two sets of legs—one male, one female.

"Oh, I'm fine, thank you," she called, wishing they would just get lost.

Straightening up, she found herself face-to-face with an older couple: a man with a full beard and a skinny lady who looked as though she could use a good burrito deluxe dinner.

Phoebe dangled the small sack of dirt before their curious eyes. "Clumsy me," she said, "I just dropped this on the ground. But I found it. No problem. Off I go."

"Wait." The man lifted his chin. "What is that on your hand?"

Quickly Phoebe stashed the pouch of dirt into her pocket. Whoops! She was supposed to remember not to go showing off her manicure.

"Her fingers!" the skinny woman cried.

Phoebe sighed. Did they have to freak out over some nail polish?

"Crimson nails!" the woman shrieked. "I saw nails the color of blood! The girl is riddled with sickness."

"I am not sick!" Phoebe protested.

"Then show us!" the man demanded. "Let us see for ourselves."

Was it better to show them or just hightail it out of there? Phoebe had a feeling that if she ran, that would just prove to them that there was something weird about her nails. Besides, other curious villagers were gathering around her. The odds weren't so hot that she'd actually get away.

Phoebe held out her hands. That darned manicure had really held up! Some of the polish was scratched and chipped from the back-

breaking work she'd been doing, but overall
her nails were dark red, a crimson nightmare.

An angry buzz rippled through the crowd.
"Stand back," the bearded man shouted, pulling
his wife away. "She has the plague. A plague
upon us! She will be the death of us all!"

Phoebe buried her hands in the deep pockets of Prudence's cloak. "I'm not sick," she said
quickly. "It's just . . . I was picking berries and
my fingers got all red from the juice." She
turned to a young woman in the crowd and
looked her straight in the eye. "You know how
that happens? I hate it. Berry juice everywhere."

"What sort of berries are harvested in
springtime?" asked a man from the back of the
crowd.

Phoebe turned toward him and gasped. Was
that a flash of green on his skin?

Yes! A hideous green.

It was the demon, standing right in the mob.
Glaring at Phoebe, he shouted, "It is not a sick-
ness we look upon, but the very face of evil.
She is a witch!"

"Witch?" A gasp echoed through the crowd.

The demon in human form stepped forward.
"Lock her in the stocks," he shouted, "so that she
may be tried for the evil of witchcraft!"

"Hold on!" Phoebe shouted. "This is so
unfair!"

But no one was listening. The crowd shifted,

and Phoebe stepped back as they advanced on her. This was getting seriously scary.

"Hey, can't we talk about this?" Phoebe asked.

A tall man stepped out of the crowd and grabbed Phoebe by the arm. Phoebe struggled to break free, but he was too strong. A moment later he was helped by another villager who clamped his hands on her other elbow. Her boots slid across the ground as they dragged her down the road.

Phoebe's heart was pounding. What were they going to do with her?

Then she saw the stocks. Their wooden frames and iron clamps looked strong and unforgiving.

If they locked her in there, she wouldn't have a chance, especially with the green demon around to incite the crowd. There would be no escape. No demon-banishing. No returning home.

Phoebe shut her eyes. She couldn't bear to look at the waiting stocks.

"Witch!" someone shouted.

"Devil's spawn!" cried another.

She opened her eyes as she felt something hit her. Oh, gross! Someone had actually thrown an egg.

But drippy eggs were the least of her problems. She was trapped, totally vulnerable and terrifyingly alone.

CHAPTER
11

Phoebe glared from one man to another as they dragged her closer to the stocks. She could feel her pulse racing, a sure sign that panic was setting in.

But she couldn't let these old-school buffoons win. She had twenty-first century know-how on her side, didn't she? If only she'd brought a cell phone through the time rift. You could always count on a ringing cell phone for an annoying interruption.

Then she remembered the spices in her pocket. Archaic, yes, but they might provide a reasonable distraction.

The man on her right was holding her upper arm, but her hand was free. She dipped it into her pocket and felt around inside. There were nutmeg kernels, salt crystals, and . . . ground pepper.

She felt for the pepper sack with its ribbon tie. Carefully, slowly, her fingers worked the knot loose and slipped the ribbon away. Perfect.

They reached the stocks, and one man got to work unfastening the bolts to open up the ridiculous contraption. The entire crowd watched in awe. You people don't get out much, do you? Phoebe wanted to ask them.

"Hurry up, now, Will," the tall man told the guard who was working the bolts. "We need to lock her up quickly. We can't allow the witch to work any more of her sorcery on us."

Closing her hand around the pouch in her pocket, Phoebe turned her face up to the guard at her side. "My advice?" she said sweetly. "If you're afraid of magic, don't mess with a Charmed One!"

She pulled the sack of pepper out of her pocket and tossed it into his face. She was aiming for his eyes, but his nose would do, too.

A murmur of shock rippled through the crowd as the guard recoiled. He was sneezing furiously and rubbing his eyes.

"Will, are you all right?" a woman called.

"The witch has blinded me!" he bellowed.

"Magic dust!" someone gasped. "It came from her crimson fingers!"

The other guard actually ducked behind the stocks. "Don't hurt me, witch! I beg you."

"Not today," Phoebe muttered under her breath. "I'm all out of magic dust." Before the smell of pepper could give her away, Phoebe tore away from the angry pack and ran like crazy.

Hours later Phoebe was hunkered down in the underbrush by the spring. Up the hill she could just make out the torches of the angry villagers clustered outside Prudence's cottage.

She knew that they had come for her.

Well, at least Prudence wouldn't be lying when she said she didn't know where Phoebe was. Phoebe had stayed away from the cottage all afternoon, realizing that a witch hunt was inevitable. It took them long enough to get here. Maybe the tall guy had some trouble getting the pepper out of his hair.

Phoebe moved as close as she dared, hiding behind an oak tree. From here it looked as if a few of the villagers had gone inside to search the cottage.

Suddenly Phoebe had a new worry. What if the searchers found *The Book of Shadows*? They might destroy it! It would be lost to the generations of witches in her family. Definitely not how she wanted to change the past and affect the future. Plus, Prudence would be in serious trouble, too.

Phoebe's heart hammered. What would happen to little, defenseless Cassandra if the mob went after her mother?

"They *can't* find the book," Phoebe murmured to herself, as if saying the words would make them true. *"They cannot find it!"*

Long moments later Phoebe saw the crowd move on. They seemed disappointed. Chances were, they hadn't found anything, but Phoebe wanted to be sure. She waited until the mob was completely out of sight, then crept over to the cottage. She went up to the small window and peered inside the common room.

Prudence was there, sipping root tea and rocking Cassandra in her arms. Phoebe nearly collapsed with relief. If Prudence and Cassandra were safe, then so was the book.

Something about the sight of the mother and daughter struck Phoebe right in her heart. Cassandra was a little old to be held that way, but she'd probably been frightened by the mob. And wasn't it surprising that Prudence, for all of her mood swings, was such a devoted mom? Somehow seeing Prudence and Cassandra together this way made Phoebe feel all choked up and sentimental. She wished she'd had more time with her own mom, but she also felt good, knowing that a mother and daughter in her distant family could be together to comfort each other.

Phoebe stepped back from the cabin. She knew she couldn't go inside. There was no telling when the villagers might double back. Besides, just seeing Phoebe could bring out the monster in Prudence again.

And speaking of monsters, there was still the demon to banish.

Earlier Phoebe had sneaked into the barn, where she'd hidden most of the ingredients for her spell. Now she had her collection in her pockets: a thimble, the pouch of soil, a tea leaf, a nutmeg kernel, and two flat stones. There were just two more items on the list: a feather and some Queen Anne's lace.

Time to finish off my collection and go for it.

"Buuk! B-buk!" a chicken clucked as Phoebe approached the henhouse.

"Oh, shoosh," she whispered. She didn't want the whole flock to announce that she was here, but she did need a feather.

She found one wedged into a splintered board. "It's a pleasure doing business with you," she said, yanking it out.

Then she was off, heading back into the dark woods again. From her distant Girl Scout days she remembered that Queen Anne's lace often grew wild in the fields and close to hedges. She figured she would recognize the delicate off-white flower when she saw it.

Fortunately, the half-moon in the sky was bright enough to light parts of the ground. Watching for strangers, Phoebe stayed close to the edge of the forest. The woods, she figured, were her best hideout. Standing in the middle of an open field, silhouetted by moonlight, would not be too smart.

Phoebe stepped over roots and rocks, and walked into a few thorny bushes that caught at her long skirts. An owl called and she jumped, nearly scared out of her skin. She saw thistle and heather and something that looked a lot like poison ivy, but no Queen Anne's lace.

Up ahead she saw an old log covered with moss and mushrooms. Fertile ground—maybe a good place to find an elusive plant. When she reached the fat log, she noticed a light in the distance.

A light in the middle of the woods?

Phoebe squinted through the trees and saw an open fire. Someone was leaning close to it, tending it with a stick. She stepped around the log and peered around a birch tree. Another figure sat by the fire, a hooded cloak covering his or her features.

Then she heard the voices—male voices.

The man with the stick turned and Phoebe recognized him. Hugh! What was he doing here? And to whom was he talking?

Phoebe worked her way around the clearing. Sneaking from tree to tree, she crept off to the side and pressed herself against a wide oak tree. This time, when she swung around, she saw the face under the hood.

The demon! The green demon was sitting with Hugh!

CHAPTER
12

Clink!

Two billiard balls crashed together and flew off to opposite corners of the green felt table. Piper hunkered down expectantly as the eight ball fell into the corner pocket. "Woo-hoo! I win!"

"No, man," a guy in a red leather jacket called from a nearby table. "Sinking the eight ball is bad luck."

Piper laughed, long and hard. Who needs luck when you've got wicked powers? she thought.

The guy in the red jacket looked confused, but Prue just raised an eyebrow at her.

Actually, Piper knew that although she felt totally exhilarated, she still didn't have a clue as to what her new powers might be. Not the way Prue did when it happened to her.

Stepping back as Prue took a shot, Piper felt a stab of doubt. What if she didn't get that warlock's powers after all? What if she'd been cheated? She didn't even want to think about it, and she didn't want to say anything to Prue—not yet.

"You know," Prue said, "we should do this more often."

Piper leaned over the table to take a shot. "You're not talking about playing pool, are you?"

"No, I'm not." She lowered her voice so that no one else would hear. "I'm talking about warlocks. Think about it, Piper. Maybe it's our destiny. Maybe we're supposed to destroy warlocks and steal their powers. We *are* the Charmed Ones, right?"

"With Phoebe," Piper reminded her sister. "The *three* of us are the Charmed Ones."

"Who's Phoebe?" Prue asked.

Piper laughed. "Our sister, stupid. Like you don't remember."

Prue shot a ball into the side pocket, then straightened. "I've got a brilliant idea. Let's blow out of here and hit the book again. I'm sure we can find some more very interesting stuff to do in there."

"Hit the books? You girls in college?" Red Jacket asked.

Prue rolled her eyes and motioned for Piper to follow her.

They ducked into the hallway and went into the corridor by the cigarette machine. Then they touched hands and their bodies went flat and folded into smaller and smaller and smaller pieces. . . .

The next thing Piper saw was her sister unfolding. She opened up into a 2-D image, then became herself again in the attic of Halliwell Manor.

"Show-off," Piper said, shaking off Prue's hand.

"Just call it the origami express." Prue grinned.

But Piper was not amused. She didn't really want to be here, in the house, and suddenly she felt angry. Maybe it was being back in the dingy old attic. Cobwebs hung from the beams. The floor was caked in dust, and melted wax had hardened in pools here and there. She pushed aside a box, picked up a dress on a hanger, and used it to wipe off a spot to sit.

Prue was already standing at *The Book of Shadows*, running her fingers over a page as if the whole thing tickled her. The book was like an addiction to her now.

"As I was saying," Prue murmured, "I think we're onto something with this warlock stuff. I really do. But something else just hit me. Why should we limit our power-theft to warlocks?"

"Because you can't steal power from a loaf of bread?" Piper quipped.

"I mean, why don't we go after witches, too?" Prue proposed.

Piper frowned. "You mean, good witches—like us?"

That made Prue laugh. "Piper, when was the last time you looked at yourself in the mirror?"

Piper looked down at her clothes: a black full-length skirt, black lace blouse, and leather jacket. "What's wrong with the way I'm dressed?"

"Clothes don't make the witch, Piper. It's what we're doing. We're not exactly on the straight and narrow anymore."

Piper wasn't sure she liked what she was hearing, but she didn't want to argue with Prue again. Instead, she stood up and walked over to *The Book of Shadows*. Maybe they needed to find a new spell. Something that would clear the cobwebs from the attic and from her mind.

"The point is," Prue went on, "warlocks are so limited. Witches have much more interesting skills—definitely worth stealing."

Piper leafed through the book, flipping past disgusting spells and nauseating recipes: spells for cursing enemies, recipes to make children sicken. Something just wasn't right. *The Book of Shadows* wasn't supposed to include black magic. Piper was sure of that, but there it was. Had the evil just appeared there? Or had it been there all along? When she tried to straighten it out in her mind, her brain felt sort of pinched. Or maybe she was just getting a headache.

She turned the page and found a spell to take away a witch's powers. The spell required a live human heart.

She shuddered. "Where did all this gruesome stuff come from? Since when do we work with human and animal parts."

"I don't know," Prue said. She started pacing, a sure sign of irritation.

"This other spell calls for the eye of a cat," Piper pointed out, wincing as she thought of their own beloved Siamese. "I don't think Kit would approve."

"Who cares?" Prue snapped. "And you're going off on a tangent again, Piper. You need to focus. Think of good witches. Do we know any good witches whose power we can take?"

"Phoebe," Piper answered automatically.

"Who's Phoebe?" Prue asked.

This time Piper no longer had an answer to the question. Wait a minute, she thought. Who *is* Phoebe?

CHAPTER
13

Phoebe couldn't believe what she was seeing. Her pulse hammered as she pressed her cheek to the bark of the tree, straining to hear the low, evil voices. Hugh was meeting with the demon. Had he been a part of the demon's plan from the beginning?

Hugh tossed a small log on the fire, then dropped his head like a sad child. "I did everything you told me to do. I gave Prudence the root tea—cup after cup. But the spell isn't working. Prudence should have completely turned to the dark side by now, but there are moments of goodness still."

The tea!

Phoebe bit her lip. From the first day she'd been there, Hugh had been insisting that

Prudence drink the root tea, a tea that was part of a spell. Maybe that explained Prudence's bizarre mood swings.

"The root tea has not been entirely unsuccessful," the demon said with a smug smile. "She is adding to *The Book of Shadows*. Every spell she adds while under its influence is a spell of black magic."

Phoebe felt nauseated at the thought of the demon using Prudence to put black magic into *The Book of Shadows*. It was also pretty revolting that she'd believed what Hugh and the demon wanted her to believe: that Prudence was into black magic—that her ancestor was her enemy.

The truth was that Prudence was enspelled and needed Phoebe's help—and Phoebe had almost failed her.

"Then there's the problem of Phoebe," Hugh went on. "What do we need her for? Why did you bring her here at all?"

The demon laughed. "I couldn't resist. It's going to be a delight to watch. Phoebe will be her own undoing. You have forgotten, I am a time demon. Spreading evil throughout time is my specialty.

"Your attentions to Phoebe have made the lovely Prudence quite jealous," the demon went on. "She is hideously ugly with jealousy. Phoebe is helping turn Prudence evil without even knowing it! Once Prudence is evil, her spawn will be evil, too. The darkness will infect Cassandra, who will then corrupt her daughter, and so on through the generations. Every one of the Charmed Ones will be soldiers of the dark instead of witches of the light."

Phoebe gripped the tree, her nails digging into the bark as the big ugly picture sank in. Gram. Her mother. Piper and Prue. . . . All the Halliwell women would be evil, horrible, miserable creatures.

And me, too, Phoebe realized. Her knees were shaking under her, and she knew that it wasn't from the cold night air.

"It is time to take the next step," the demon told Hugh. "A human sacrifice is in order. I have already sent Prudence the spell in a dream, but she is hesitating. You must strengthen your own spell over her. Then you must instruct her to take an innocent life."

Hugh smiled. "But whom shall she sacrifice?"

The demon returned his smile. "Phoebe Halliwell is the obvious choice, don't you think?"

Kill *me?* Phoebe pressed her cheek against the bark, trying to be still and silent.

Hugh got to his feet and approached the fire. He took something from a leather pouch that hung at his waist and threw it into the flames. Then he raised his arms and began to chant in strange words that Phoebe didn't recognize. She watched, astounded, as an image of Prudence sleeping peacefully flickered in the center of the fire while Hugh continued to chant.

He's a warlock! Phoebe realized, her stomach churning with disgust. How could I have missed that? Well, for one thing, he somehow managed to disguise all the normal warlock signs.

The image in the flames vanished, and Hugh turned to the demon. "The spell is in place, and your will shall be done," he said. "Prudence will kill before the morrow."

Phoebe held her breath as she edged away from the clearing. She couldn't let them hear her. She nearly tripped over a fallen log but caught herself at the last minute. Then, when she was a safe distance away, she ran.

Her heavy cloak billowed behind her as she raced along the trail. She couldn't get the image of those two monsters out of her head— the warlock Hugh talking over the fire to the hideous demon. She had suspected that the demon had brought her here for a reason, that she was being set up for something evil. But she'd never imagined it would be to help turn her whole line of ancestors to black magic.

I have to stop this from happening, Phoebe thought. If only she could let Prue and Piper know what was going on, what was at stake. But how could she send a message to the future?

Anything I do now will have an effect on the future, Phoebe reminded herself. She reached the end of the woods and slowed to a brisk walk. Okay, so maybe I should engrave a message on a stone and hope one of them sees it. Or send a letter—except there's no mail system yet.

She mulled over the problem all the way back to Prudence's cottage. Peering into the window, she saw that the common room was dark and empty. Phoebe slipped inside and quietly perused the cottage. Prudence and Cassandra were asleep in the back room. Not quite sure what to do next, Phoebe climbed onto a chair and pulled *The Book of Shadows* from its spot in the rafters.

By the light of a single candle, Phoebe searched the book. She remembered that old Green Face had called himself a time demon. Maybe she could find some helpful info about that.

But as she reached the end of the written spells, she realized her search was useless.

Another dead end, Phoebe thought, staring at the open book. She turned back to a familiar page with a bright drawing of a woman with flowers in her hair. It was a page she'd always loved, back in the comfort of the attic at Halliwell Manor.

Wait. Ohhh, wait! Phoebe thought. If this page made it through the ages and into the hands of the Halliwell sisters, then anything Phoebe wrote right now would appear in *The Book of Shadows* hundreds of years in the future!

Phoebe flipped to the empty pages at the back and went to the sideboard to grab Prudence's writing quill and ink pot. With a deep breath, she dipped the quill into the ink and began to write:

"This is a (frantic!) message to Piper and Prue: Help! It's me, Phoebe. . . ."

"You know, a witch-hunt isn't a bad idea at all," Piper said, snapping onto Prue's line of thinking. "Let's make a list of all the witches we know with the coolest powers. Then we can go after them in order. You know, prioritize them."

"Exactly." Prue's blue eyes flashed with interest. "You make the list. I'll hit the book for a juicy, wicked spell." She laughed, but it came out more as a cackle. The sound reminded Piper of a crow cawing from high in a tree.

"Something mean and rotten," Piper agreed. Suddenly she was laughing along with Prue, laughing so hard she couldn't go on.

Prue stopped short when she turned the page. "Whoa."

"What is it?" Piper asked.

Prue's eyes opened wide as she stared at *The Book of Shadows*. "There's a message here and it's . . . it's writing itself." She waved her sister over with her hands. "Right now. Look!" She grabbed Piper's sleeve and yanked her over to see the book.

Piper couldn't believe it. Words were scrawling themselves onto the page in black ink. She read aloud: "'This is a frantic message to Piper and Prue.' How weird is that? And that handwriting is familiar."

"You're right." Prue squinted. "Very weird."

"Wait." Piper watched in amazement as the words scrolled on. "It's a message from— Phoebe."

"Phoebe?" Prue repeated.

In a flash Piper's memory came flooding back: Phoebe as a little girl and then as a teenager. Phoebe making Piper laugh like no one else. Phoebe always being one of the two people she loved best. Phoebe discovering *The Book of Shadows*. And finally, Phoebe following a warlock down an alley and disappearing from their lives.

And now this message . . .

"She's alive!" Piper threw an arm around Prue's shoulders and started jumping up and down. "Phoebe is alive!"

CHAPTER
14

Standing close together, Piper and Prue watched in amazement as the message scrawled itself into the book.

This is a (frantic!) message to Piper and Prue:

Help! It's me, Phoebe, and I'm alive and kicking in Salem, Massachusetts.

Yes, Salem, land of the witch-hunt. I've been told the year is 1676, and I'm staying with this chick named Prudence who is actually our ancestor (and, I guess, your namesake, Prue). She's not a lot of help, though, since she's under an evil spell.

The thing is, that warlock who attacked us is actually a time demon (whatever that

means), and he sucked me through a por-
tal—some kind of time rift or something—
and here I am.

The demon is here, too, planting seeds
of evil to ruin our family. Oh, yeah—he's
got a warlock helping him. Anyway, here I
am up a river of evil without a good witch
in sight—and I'm drowning! HELP!

Love you guys! And I miss you!
Phoebe

"Whoa," Piper slowly whispered. Reading
Phoebe's words had snapped her out of her
passion to steal someone else's power, and it
had cleared a lot of the haze in her mind.

Suddenly the attic didn't look so bad. There
were just a few cobwebs and some melted
wax—nothing that a broom and dustpan
couldn't fix.

And Prue . . . Turning to her sister, Piper no
longer felt the anger and jealousy that had
overcome her lately. Prue was her sister. Yes,
sometimes she was bossy, but her heart was
always, always in the right place. Well, maybe
not during the past few days, but usually.

" 'Whoa' is right," Prue said. "Do you realize
what's happened to us? Ever since Phoebe disappeared, we've been slipping into this black
abyss. But now, I don't know, maybe it's just
knowing that she's still alive . . . somehow I feel
better again."

"I know what you mean," Piper admitted.

"How could we forget that we're the Charmed Ones?" Prue asked, her brow knit with concern.

"We were incomplete without Phoebe. But it's more than that. We've been getting into some pretty nasty stuff." Piper shivered. "I feel sort of . . . dirty."

"Well, cleanse your mind and start thinking of a way to help Phoebe. We've got work to do." Prue turned back the pages of *The Book of Shadows*. "I wonder if there's a spell in here to deal with that time demon. Let's see."

It didn't take long to find a reference to the time demon. According to the book, his name was Falcroft.

" 'Falcroft is very powerful, very evil,' " Piper read from the book. " 'He constantly tries to wreak havoc in the past, present, and future.' "

"At the moment he seems to be doing a great job," Prue observed. She put her hands on her hips. "So he's the one who's brought this evil into our lives. Because of the things he's done, we've been falling into black magic."

Piper shook her head. "This is really scary. If we don't banish him, things will never return to normal. His plan to corrupt the future—and our present—will succeed."

A rueful look lit Prue's eyes. "So many innocent people will get hurt."

"And we won't even be ourselves," Piper added.

Pacing nervously, Prue ran her fingers through her dark hair. "So we know the demon's name: Falcroft. Maybe we should summon him."

"Summon a demon?" Piper winced. "Oh, sure. Let's just ask him over for dinner or something."

"More like, or something." Prue went back to *The Book of Shadows.* "I think there's a spell in here that will help us summon him."

"I'm not sure that's the smartest thing to do right now," Piper told her sister. "I mean, once we summon him, what do we do with him?"

Prue frowned. "Good question."

The candle had burned down to a stub, but Phoebe was still reading by its light in the common room of Prudence's cottage. She had finished her letter to her sisters an hour earlier but had stayed up to study the demon-banishing spell. She had all the ingredients but one, and she was short one witch. Still, she wanted to make sure she'd memorized every word. A girl's got to be prepared.

Her head bowed over the table, Phoebe froze when she heard something stirring.

Prudence stood in the bedroom doorway.

"They told me you were a witch, but I knew they were wrong." Prudence's eyes were rimmed with dark circles. Her cheeks looked thin and hollow and the dim light. "You're an evil warlock. A warlock who's come to steal my powers—and my man."

"Oh, honey, that is so wrong," Phoebe said earnestly. She pushed back the chair to stand up, and Prudence went stiff with fear.

Whipping out her hand, Prudence pointed to Phoebe with a fierce look of concentration. Phoebe felt a strange resistance in the air, but it didn't stop her from standing up and taking a step toward Prudence.

Prudence gasped, staring at her hand. "Why isn't it working?"

Phoebe blinked. She realized Prudence had tried to use telekinesis to stop her, but Prudence's powers hadn't worked, probably because Phoebe was a Charmed One.

"My powers are gone!" Prudence's face twisted in agony. "It's all because of you—you and your evil!"

"No, no, wait a sec. I *am* a witch. Just not the kind that you think." Phoebe held up her hands to calm the other woman, but Prudence saw the movement as an attack. She staggered back, bumping into the sideboard.

Prudence's voice rose to a hysterical pitch. "You have come here to take everything from me!"

"That's not true." Phoebe moved toward her slowly. "If you'll let me, I'd like to help you."

"No, stop!" Prudence fell back, groping the counter behind her. When she raised her hand, she was holding a long, sharp hunting knife.

The blade glinted in the candlelight. Phoebe swallowed hard. What had Hugh said? "The spell is in place. Prudence will kill before the morrow."

"You've given me no choice," Prudence said, raising the knife. Her voice was almost a whisper, but there was a wildness in her eyes that made Phoebe tremble. "I have to kill you."

CHAPTER
15

Please, don't do this!" Phoebe cried.

But Prudence's blue eyes were lit with madness. The knife's blade sliced down toward Phoebe's chest.

This is the end, Phoebe realized. The end of me. The end of future generations of good witches. It's all over now.

But the blade never reached her skin. Prudence pulled her arm back, and the knife clattered to the floor. Then she dropped to her knees and burst into tears.

"I can't do it," she sobbed. "I can't kill you."

Phoebe took a deep breath. She was still alive. Alive was good. Lucky for her, Prudence's mood had changed mid-knife swing. Phoebe knelt beside Prudence and put a hand on her shoulder.

"Don't touch me," Prudence warned. "I'm enchanted. Under a spell. There's no telling what I might do to you."

"I know all that," Phoebe said.

Prudence gave her a look of amazement.

"Listen," she told Prudence, "none of this is your fault. Hugh put a spell on you. He's a warlock, working with this gruesome demon to poison your powers and ruin the magic powers of your descendants."

Phoebe jumped up and went to *The Book of Shadows*. It was still open to the demon-banishing spell. Quickly, she leafed through the book. There had to be a way to break Hugh's enchantment. Remembering something she'd seen there earlier, Phoebe flipped back and smiled at what she read: "A Spell to Splinter Enchantment."

"Okay, Prudence, you're going to be all better in a second." Phoebe gathered candles and ingredients for the spell. She found the gold crescent-moon charm that had once belonged to Melinda, Prudence's mother. That would work as something that the "Enchanted One" valued. She picked up Cassandra's rag doll to use as a "sign of family." Then she took a linen napkin from Hugh's place at the table as "an evil thing to cast away."

Phoebe sat on the floor opposite Prudence. She placed the doll in Prudence's lap, then put the gold charm and napkin in a bowl between them. When the candles were lit, she reached across and took the other woman's hands.

"You're going to have to say this with me, okay?"

Tears sparkled in Prudence's blue eyes, but she nodded.

Phoebe glanced over at *The Book of Shadows* and recited:

> "Day to night,
> Night to day,
> Break the spell,
> Cast it away."

Across from her, Prudence was still as a stone. "Come on, Prudence! Wake up and smell the root tea."

Prudence glanced up, then nodded wearily.

"Okay, let's try it again." Phoebe squeezed her hands, and together they chanted.

" 'Day to night, Night to day, Break the spell, Cast it away. Day to night, night to day, break the spell . . .' "

A bright golden light encircled both women. It flashed once, then vanished. Phoebe saw that the linen napkin was gone, too. She looked across at Prudence, who gave her a small smile. Her eyes were clear and bright now, her face without shadows or dark lines.

"The enchantment is gone," Prudence said, the joy returning to her voice. She blew out the candles, then reached across to give Phoebe a hug.

Phoebe closed her eyes as she squeezed Prudence tight. It felt so good to be with a friend for the first time in days. "Welcome back to the land of light," she said quietly.

Prudence leaned back and smiled. "Now, Phoebe Halliwell, help me clear the fog from my eyes. Tell me who you really are and why you're here."

Phoebe handed the crescent-moon charm back to Prudence. "First, you'll want to keep this in a safe place. I know it's special to you."

"Yes, it belonged to my mother." Prudence squeezed the charm in the palm of one hand and went pale. Suddenly her eyes were glassy and distant.

"Prudence?" Phoebe touched her arm gently. "What's wrong?"

"A vision." She shuddered, obviously frightened.

"What was it? Tell me."

Prudence took a deep breath. "No, we shouldn't speak of it." She turned away to light a fire in the fireplace. "There's no time for details. I sense that we have so much to do."

Already the morning sun had begun to glow in the window. As the women sat at the table, Phoebe spoke quickly about the demon and the time rift and the future generations of Charmed Ones. They also spoke about Hugh.

"I realize he's in thick with the demon," Prudence said, "but it's hard to believe him a warlock. He was once a kind, gentle man. To know he's fallen into evil is truly a heartbreak."

"There may be hope for him," Phoebe said. "But first we've got to banish that demon. There's a spell for it, and I've already collected everything we need. Well, almost everything. Where in the world do you find Queen Anne's lace around here?"

Prudence laughed as she sliced off a few slabs of bread. "I do believe there's some growing down by the spring."

"And I traipsed all the way out to the woods for it."

Prudence went to the fireplace and put the bread on the warming rack on the fire. "I know just where to find it. But first, there's Cassandra. I will need to keep her safe during the next few days." She disappeared into the bedroom and called her daughter's name.

Within minutes Cassandra was dressed and fed and rubbing her eyes in early-morning confusion. "Why am I going to visit Miss Mary Pierce?" she asked in a squeaky voice. "Didn't we visit her just a few days ago?"

"She is a good friend," Prudence said emphatically. With a gentle touch, she tied her daughter's bonnet and handed her a parcel of butter. "You may bring her this. I'm sure Mary will be delighted to see you again."

Prudence leaned down and gave her daughter a kiss and a warm hug. "Goodbye, my dear. I do love you." She touched her daughter's cheek, then opened the door.

As she closed it, Phoebe noticed her blinking back tears. "Prudence, what did you see in that vision?"

Prudence just shook her head. "Have you forgotten the first business of the day?" She opened *The Book of Shadows* to the demon-banishing spell and placed a flower in the page to mark it. "Why don't you start setting out all the ingredients you've assembled? I will walk down to the spring in search of the Queen Anne's lace."

"All right, but shake a leg, okay? We're up against a wall here." Phoebe picked up her cloak to remove the valuable pouches from its pockets. She felt a new urgency, as if time were suddenly running out.

"Shake a leg?" Prudence asked. "You do have the oddest manner of speech." She grabbed a shawl and headed out the door.

"Prue!" Piper shouted out from the attic. "I found it! It's perfect!" She cradled a delicate blown-glass ornament in her hand—a sphere with tiny glass stars that rolled around inside. The Christmas ornament had been a favorite of the three girls as they'd grown up. Every year as they had decorated the tree, they'd argued about who would get to hang the ornament. This would be perfect.

When the spell called for "A delicate object of contention," both Prue and Piper had been baffled. But Piper had set her mind to what that object might be, and since they couldn't really use any of their boyfriends from high school, the ornament was the next thing that came to her.

Hearing Prue's footsteps on the stairs, Piper tucked a cloth into the clay bowl and gently placed the ornament on top of it.

"I got lucky, too," Prue called as she rushed into the attic. In her arms she held a rose, an egg, and a muddy old brick from the backyard. One by one, she set the items down on the low table.

"That should do it," Piper said, checking the list. "Just remind me, what are we going to do when we get the demon here?"

"You're going to freeze him, and I'm going to kick him into another astral plane."

Piper frowned. "I hope you're feeling super-strong today."

Prue knelt at the table to reorganize the ingredients for the spell. "Trust me," she said, picking up the glass ornament. "This is going to be—"

Crunch.

Piper had a sick feeling in her stomach. "What was that?"

"The ornament!" Prue's face turned white as she stared down at the floor. "It rolled out of my hand."

The ornament was shattered. Tiny pieces of glass lay scattered on the floor.

"Oh, no!" Piper moaned in frustration. "Now what are we going to do?"

"I—I don't know," Prue yelled.

Piper rubbed her temples. "We had everything ready a minute ago. If we could only go back one minute—"

Whoooosh!

Strange sounds shot out of Piper's mouth, and she felt herself stepping back like a robot. Prue also made some weird sounds, then held up her hand as the shards of glass on the floor scrambled together, formed a ball, then leaped back into Prue's hand.

Whooosh!

Just as quickly as the episode began, it ended—with Prue holding the perfect ornament, still in one piece.

"Unbelievable," Prue said, staring at the ornament. She turned to Piper, and the glass ball started to tip again.

Piper rushed forward. "I'll take care of that," she said, cradling the ornament with two hands.

Prue stood up, wiping her hands on her long, black dress. "Did you do that? That whole backward-time thing?"

Piper smiled. "I think so." Gently Piper placed the ornament in the bowl. "Could that be the new power I got from that warlock?"

"Piper," Prue exclaimed. "You've gained the power to turn back time! It's exactly what we need to rescue Phoebe!"

CHAPTER
16

Prue was pacing again, her black skirt swaying behind her. "This changes everything! Now you can take us back in time to 1676."

Piper hoped she could get them to the right year. After all, turning back time was a new power for her and they couldn't indulge in a practice run.

"And with my new powers I can zip us over to Massachusetts." Prue folded her arms. "It's perfect."

"But what if we do something that alters history in, like, this huge, devastating way?" Piper asked.

"We'll have to be very careful to avoid just that," Prue acknowledged. "It's freaky tampering with the chain of events, but the demon's

151

already doing that, and we have to stop him. This is the only way to defeat him and rescue Phoebe."

Pressing a new candle into a clay holder, Piper noticed her sister's outfit: a long, black velvet dress and velvet cloak. "You're looking like the Wicked Witch of the West. You'll be a huge hit in Salem."

Prue eyed her skeptically. "And when did you decide to go Goth? Could you get any darker with that eye shadow?"

Piper laughed. "Don't be shy. Tell me what you really think." It was good to be joking with her sister again. During these past few days their relationship had been so completely infected with evil. Now, finally, they were back on track.

The two sisters joined hands. "Please, please, let this work," Piper murmured.

"Focus on Phoebe," Prue told her. "On Salem Village in Massachusetts. Because we are going to teleport back to 1676."

Whoooosh!

As Piper concentrated on the year 1676 she saw Prue's body go flat and begin to fold into smaller pieces. Then, suddenly, her whole world exploded into magnificent pinpoints of light.

Prudence's cottage was eerily quiet as Phoebe waited for her to return. She had everything for the spell. All the ingredients were lined up in a semicircle around the fireplace. Since this spell required the witch to toss the ingredients into a fire, Phoebe figured that the fireplace would be the safest way to do it.

The only things missing were the Queen Anne's lace and Prudence. Where was she? Every second was critical.

"Here it is," Prudence called as the door creaked open.

"At last," Phoebe sighed. "I was beginning to think you had to teleport yourself to Tahiti to get it."

"What's Tahiti?" Prudence asked.

Phoebe frowned. "I'll explain later. Help me light these candles and let's get this spell on the road."

Together they lit two candles and knelt on opposite sides of the hearth. Phoebe turned to *The Book of Shadows*, which sat on the floor beside her, and began to read aloud.

"Friends of light and sister sun,
    Winter moon and summer shower . . ."

Slam! The door banged open.

Phoebe blinked and looked up. Hugh Montgomery stood in the doorway, staring at them.

"Hugh!" Prudence hitched up her skirt and rushed over to him. "My goodness, are you feeling poorly? You look dreadfully pale."

Hugh's beady eyes glittered with suspicion. "My health is fine," he answered, staring at Phoebe. "If I am pale, it is only because I have just seen a witch."

No point denying it now, Phoebe decided. She stood up. "You rang?"

"Oh, Hugh, I do believe you misunderstand the situation," Prudence began. "We were just . . . just tending the fire and—"

"I cannot believe what I'm seeing!" Hugh exclaimed.

"Please, be calm." Prudence shushed him.

"I will not! And look what's happened to you, suddenly with a mind and a will of your own!" All pretense of goodness had slipped away from him. As he scowled at Prudence, the monster within began to show its deadly teeth. "You've turned back to the other side!"

Prudence was still for a moment, almost stunned.

"Look," Phoebe told Hugh, "why don't you just save your sweet butt and hightail it out of here? Otherwise, it's not going to be a pretty sight."

Furious, Hugh spun toward Phoebe and pointed to the fireplace. A fireball arose and crashed at her feet.

"Whoa!" Phoebe jumped back as sparks and smoke filled the air. He'd missed but he'd come too close.

Phoebe knew he was an evil sexist warlock

pig, but somehow she hadn't expected him to hurl fireballs.

"Hugh, stop it right now!" Prudence ordered.

Still seething, Hugh summoned a second fireball from the hearth and cast this one at Prudence.

Immediately her hands flew up to stop it. But the ball of fire split into a fiery rope, which wound itself around Prudence in a flaming spiral.

"Your powers are weak," Hugh said, scoffing at Prudence. "Too little practice, my dear, and far too much root tea." With a twirl of his finger, he tightened the coils around Prudence.

"Hugh . . . stop!" she cried out as flames licked at her shoulders.

"Turn off the heat, you idiot!" Phoebe screamed at him.

Pinpoints of light danced before Piper's eyes. They turned into a square of light, then unfolded to a rectangle and kept unfolding until it was a flat version of Prue. Piper could feel the same changes in herself as she watched her sister go 3-D and start to move.

Prue put her hands on her hips and glanced around them. "So this is Salem."

"Let's hope so." Piper glanced up at the thatched roof of the log cabin they'd landed in front of.

"Phoebe!" The word echoed out to them from the cottage.

Piper felt a mix of feelings: encouragement that they'd landed in the right place and fear that Phoebe was in big trouble.

Piper and Prue turned and blasted through the wooden door of the cottage. Inside, Piper felt her mouth drop open as she tried to absorb the bizarre scene.

A beautiful blond woman struggled for her life inside a coiled rope of flames. A tall, dark, and handsome warlock was controlling the coil, pulling it tighter and tighter. Phoebe stood near the woman, trying to loosen the coils with a fireplace poker, but her efforts were useless. The woman was dying—slowly, excruciatingly burning to death.

Stop! Piper thought, casting her own spell over them.

Time froze, and Phoebe rushed over and nearly collapsed in her sisters' arms.

"I am so incredibly glad to see you," Phoebe murmured into Piper's shoulder.

"We missed you, too." Piper held her two sisters close for a moment, not wanting to let go.

"Promise me you won't ever disappear like that again," Prue said, stepping back. "And before Piper's freeze ends, let's fix this picture. I take it she's the ancestor you mentioned in your letter?" She nodded at the blond woman.

Phoebe nodded at her sisters. "She's Prudence Wentworth, our great-squared grandmother. And that dude is a warlock, working for the demon. I would have sent him packing sooner, but Prudence seems to think he can be rehabilitated."

"Gotcha." Using her powers, Prue quickly unwound the flames that encircled Prudence. The fiery rope broke into pieces that scattered to the floor, now harmless embers. Prudence's entire body relaxed. "Blessed be, my sisters. Thank you."

"No problem," Prue responded. She whisked a chair over and knocked Hugh into it. As Piper watched, Prue used her power to lift a ball of yarn from the table and wind it around the man's arms, chest, and legs a gazillion times.

Phoebe reached into a jar of sticky brown goo that Prudence had labeled Salve for Burns and began smoothing it on Prudence's red, blistered skin. At once, almost miraculously, the burns began to heal.

Piper leaned in to observe. "I'm impressed," she admitted. "Did you cook up that stuff?"

Prudence blushed. "Truly I did."

Piper tapped the cover on *The Book of Shadows*. "Hope you won't mind leaving us the recipe."

"As long as I am able, I surely will," Prudence promised.

A flutter of movement caught Piper's eye. The freeze ended. Hugh kicked and flailed against his bonds, cursing, "Witches! The whole lot of you are witches!"

"These are my sisters," Phoebe said proudly, patting Piper and Prue on their backs.

Prudence nodded graciously. "Thank you for . . . for coming to our rescue. Phoebe has lifted the enchantment on me, but the demon Falcroft has been weaving chaos through time. We must find him and stop him from doing any more evil."

"Luckily, we've got everything we need for the spell that will do that," Phoebe reported. "So let's—"

"Grrrr!" An animal growl rose up from the corner of the room. Hugh was shaking violently. Smoke rose around him.

The yarn! Piper noticed. It was burning away!

Hugh broke free and bolted out of the chair. Piper was about to freeze time when Hugh blinked himself out of the picture.

She sighed. "Sorry, guys. He was too fast for me."

"It's okay." Phoebe patted her shoulder, then crossed to the door. "I know where to find him."

"I'll go with you," Prudence said, grabbing her cloak.

"Wait. You guys?" Prue interrupted. Piper

turned to see her sister already staring out the window, squinting into the distance. "I don't think you want to be running into that mob of people out there."

The others rushed to join Prue at the window. Down at the bottom of a grassy hill, Piper saw a band of villagers moving closer. Though it was morning, they were carrying torches. The sight made Phoebe very uneasy.

"The villagers," Prudence said. "I knew they'd be back. But not so soon."

The entire group swarmed to a stop as Hugh approached and spoke with their leader.

"Somehow I don't think he's singing our praises," Phoebe observed.

The villagers ran toward Prudence's cottage. As they drew closer, Piper could see the rage that swept through them. Someone in the mob started a chant, and it began to ripple stronger, louder.

"What are they saying?" Prue asked.

Phoebe frowned. "Rhymes with hitch, and it isn't the b word."

"Witch . . . witch . . . witch . . ."

The entire ground seemed to rumble as the mob approached the cottage. "Okay," Piper said. "Now this is officially scary."

Outside, the leader shouted out a message. "We have come for the witch Phoebe!"

"Phoebe?" Piper blinked in surprise. "How do they even know you?"

Phoebe bit her lip nervously. "What can I say? I make an impression."

Fists began pounding against the wooden door. Once again, the crowd began to chant. "Give us the witch! Give us the witch! Give us the witch!"

"Watch out!" Prue screamed as someone hurled a rock toward the window.

Piper ducked and Prudence, Phoebe, and Prue scrambled away from the window just seconds before the rock shattered the glass.

Another rock flew through the now-open window.

"At least the window's too small for anyone to crawl though," Phoebe pointed out.

"Come to the back room!" Prudence said. "There are no windows there."

"I don't think windows are the only problem," Piper said nervously. The cottage's heavy wooden door was shaking, the blows against it much louder now. The mob's frenzy was growing more and more intense. The chant was almost deafening now.

"The witch Phoebe must be hanged!"

CHAPTER
17

Perhaps it would be best if I spoke to them,"
Prudence said.

"Don't open that door!" Piper insisted.
"Maybe they'll just go away."

"No, they won't," Phoebe said. She went to
the door and put her hand on the bolt to slide it
open. "They've been here once before. This
time they won't go away empty-handed."

Piper placed her hand on the heavy wooden
door, holding it closed. "We are *not* going to
make it easy for them."

"Hello?" Phoebe held up her hands. "Do I
need to remind you that we are standing in a
thatched-roof house, surrounded by an angry
mob of people carrying *torches?* We are kin-
dling for the fire." She threw open the bolt.

"I'm going out there. If it gets too ugly, you can freeze time," she told Piper. "And we'll take it from there."

"This is against my better judgment," Piper announced as Phoebe threw open the door. She followed her sister out the door. There were only twenty or so people gathered in front of the cottage, but the hatred that gleamed in their eyes was so intense, she could almost feel it piercing her skin.

"There she is!" one of the men shouted. "Tie up her hands before she can cast another evil spell."

Two men stepped out of the crowd and moved toward Phoebe.

Piper and Prue quickly pulled their sister behind them, and Prudence stepped forward. "Good people of Salem, please listen to me. It would be a mistake to harm this young woman."

The two men paused, and the crowd stood silent. Piper wondered if they were reconsidering, when Hugh stepped forward.

"Prudence Wentworth speaks the truth," he said. "Phoebe is not the witch among us. The true source of evil is Prudence herself!"

A murmur rose from the crowd. It quickly turned into heated demands for "death to the witches!"

"I have proof that the Widow Wentworth is the real witch," Hugh went on. "It was she who put a spell on Phoebe when she arrived in our village—a spell to melt her clothing as a flame melts the wax of a candle."

"No way!" Phoebe said. "Prudence had nothing to do with my clothes. That was all because of you and your demon friend, Hugh. And speaking of witchcraft, who's the warlock around here?"

Hugh suddenly looked all sympathetic. "The poor child is crazy as a loon. You can't believe anything she says."

"You're all jumping to conclusions," Prue broke in. "Has this woman ever done anything to harm any of you?"

"She may have harmed a baby," Hugh said. "It was because of Prudence that Mrs. Gibbs's baby was not born. The child was on its way, but Prudence cast a spell of postponement over it. I saw this with my own eyes!"

"The child was not ready to be born," Prudence protested. "It would not have survived, but now it has a chance."

"The Widow Wentworth is the true witch! Not this feeble-minded girl," a woman called out, pointing at Phoebe.

"Prudence Wentworth is the one who must be hanged!" a burly man agreed.

"Hang her! Hang her! Hang the witch!"

Before any of the Charmed Ones had time to react, two men grabbed Prudence and began tying her hands together with rope.

"No, not a hanging," Hugh said, jumping

into the fray again. "A cleansing is in order. We must douse the evil from her completely by drowning her."

"Drowning!" the crowd echoed.

Prudence paled, looking as though she was about to faint.

Piper had seen enough. She turned to put a freeze on this whole ugly mob scene.

"Piper, no!" Prudence called to her. "Don't interfere. I had a vision . . . a vision of my destiny, I think. I was underwater, bound, unable to move or breathe. I believe it is what must be, and if I let you meddle with the events of history, the whole world will be altered. You may not even exist in the future."

Prue winced. "She might be right." She turned to Prudence. "But how do we know the vision is your destiny?"

"It was so strong," Prudence admitted. "It must be."

One guard stopped tying Prudence's hands to eye her fearfully. "Quiet, witch," he ordered.

Tears sparkled in Phoebe's eyes as she reached out to grasp Prudence's hands. "We can't let you go."

"But you must," Prudence insisted. "You cannot risk altering your futures." Already the two men were pulling her away. With a graceful nod of her head, she said goodbye to the Charmed Ones, then turned and marched off with the villagers to prepare for her "trial."

"So what are we supposed to do?" Piper asked. "Stand here while an angry mob murders our distant ancestor?"

"No! We have to save her," Phoebe insisted.

"I know you want to," Prue said. "But as long as that time demon's running around, we can't save Prudence. He can totally thwart any attempts we make. We have to take care of him first."

Piper frowned. "As much as I hate to admit it, you're right," she agreed. "Demon first, drowning later."

"And don't forget about Hugh," Phoebe reminded her sisters. "He needs to get what's coming to him, too."

"Right. But first, Falcroft. Any idea where we might find him?" Piper asked as Phoebe shoved an odd assortment of items into the pockets of her cloak.

Phoebe nodded. "I hope you're wearing your hiking boots, because we're going on a nature walk."

Piper and Prue tramped along beside their sister, crossing wide fields, then stepping over tree roots across the trail. Soon they were wending their way through the forest.

"Shhhh!" Phoebe shushed her sisters for the zillionth time. "You guys sound like a pack of elephants tromping around like that."

"If you knew exactly where it was, I could teleport us there," Prue said.

"Teleporting?" Phoebe's eyebrows lifted. "What's that? A new power? I must say I'm impressed—and a little jealous."

"Don't be," Prue said. "It's just a sordid part of our wicked future, one of the awful things that are going to happen if we don't get rid of this demon."

"Quiet," Piper warned them. "I see something through those trees." Although she couldn't see faces, one man sat facing the small bonfire. Another figure in a dark, hooded cloak was on his feet, gesturing wildly with bony arms.

Phoebe stepped closer to the light and leaned behind a tree. "That's them—Hugh and the demon. Falcroft is the skinny one wearing black from head to toe. You'll see why when we get closer. Every day is a bad skin day for that monster."

Prue pointed to a clump of bushes not far from the fire. "If we can get closer, we'll be able to hear what they're saying."

Staying low, they sneaked ahead.

"How could you be such a fool!" the demon nearly spat at Hugh. "Phoebe is supposed to be dead before Prudence is tried as a witch! How could you make such a huge mistake?"

"I didn't think it mattered," Hugh said, tossing a stick into the fire. "What's the difference? I can kill Phoebe myself."

"You defied my orders!" the demon

growled. As he swung around toward Hugh, Piper got her first glimpse of the demon's face: a huge brow ridge, swollen eyes, and scarred, seeping wounds on his gelatinous green skin. She winced. Phoebe was right. He was hideous.

Falcroft leaped forward and lifted Hugh to his feet. "You have failed as a warlock! And I cannot tolerate failure." The skin on his face was taut now, revealing rows of jagged, half-rotten teeth.

Obviously frightened, Hugh tried to step back, but Falcroft's fingers ripped into the flesh of his arms. Hugh cried out as blood seeped through his sleeves.

"You . . . you're hurting me," Hugh gasped. He squirmed and flailed but couldn't tear himself away from the demon's grip.

Falcroft grinned, his jagged teeth almost grazing Hugh's face. "Oh, that is just the beginning."

"Think we ought to interfere?" Piper whispered to her sisters.

"No!" came the instant answer.

"If you cannot obey me, then you shall still be useful," the demon told Hugh. "You shall feed me."

He gripped Hugh's shoulder with one green hand, Hugh's elbow with another. His rotting razor-edged teeth sank into the warlock's biceps.

Hugh let out a scream of anguish that made Piper's heart lurch. She knew he was an evil warlock who had as good as murdered Prudence, but still . . .

Hugh's blood dripped down the demon's chin as he contentedly munched away. Hugh was struggling, sobbing, and clearly weakening. He sank to his knees as the demon's teeth snapped through the bone.

"Girls," Phoebe whispered, "I don't think I want to see this." She hid her face in her hands.

The demon's green lips stretched wide as he opened his mouth. Piper watched in amazement as his mouth continued to stretch, until it was a huge, gaping green hole.

Then, as Hugh screamed in anguish, the demon bit off his head.

CHAPTER

18

Prue closed her eyes, but there was no blocking out the gruesome image of the demon devouring Hugh.

"Ugh!" Piper sighed and leaned into Prue. Prue touched her back gently as the wretched sounds went on—the crunching, chewing sounds.

Prue didn't want to go anywhere near the bloody scene, but she knew that Falcroft was totally engrossed in finishing off Hugh. If the Charmed Ones were going to strike, now was the time.

"Phoebe," she whispered. "Do you have all the ingredients for the spell?"

Phoebe nodded. "I put everything in one pouch." She reached into her pocket and struggled to yank something out. At last a lumpy leather pouch emerged. "Here."

"Okay," Prue said. "Let's do it."

Piper held her head down and kept her eyes to the ground. "This is gross." Her voice sounded weak. "I feel really sick."

"I know," Prue admitted. "But concentrate on the spell. Do you remember it?" Piper nodded. Phoebe had recited it for them at least ten times on the way here.

"Ready?" When Piper and Phoebe nodded, Prue linked arms with them. "Let's go."

The three Charmed Ones moved around the bushes and forged ahead. Prue struggled to keep herself from shaking. She had to be strong. Her sisters were relying on her.

"Remember the Power of Three," she said as they strode ahead.

The sound of her voice alerted the demon. He raised his bloodstained face, his bulging eyes locking on them, but the sisters kept moving toward him.

"What's this?" he asked. "Three more for dinner?"

"Have a good laugh," Phoebe said. "It's your last one."

Finally, when they were close enough to the fire, Phoebe lifted the pouch to the sky, then tossed it into the fire.

"The chant," Prue prompted. "Quickly."

Together Prue, Piper and Phoebe chanted:

"Friends of light and sister sun,
      Winter moon and summer shower,
      Send this demon back to darkness,
      Banish him, destroy his power."

Suddenly the fire flared green, purple, and bright blue. The demon's pimply green skin puffed up from his body, as though he were about to explode from inside.

Iridescent sparks began to shoot from the fire, and the demon howled in pain.

Prue squeezed her sisters' hands tighter as the flames rose up, looming over their heads.

"Should we move back?" Piper asked.

"No!" Prue shouted. "We need to stand our ground. The Power of Three will set us free!"

"The Power of Three will set us free!" they chanted together.

Red, blue, green, and purple flames shot up into the shape of a giant hand. The sisters watched in awe and fear as the hand reached far beyond the source of the fire and enveloped Falcroft. Prue blinked. Though the flames were licking right over her head, she felt no heat at all.

The giant hand lifted the demon off his feet and consumed him. His wretched, pathetic cry echoed as the spell pulled him out of time and space, depositing him in an eternal abyss.

Then it was all over. The fire, now just a few ashen logs, hissed quietly. Birds chirped outside the clearing. A squirrel scrambled up a nearby tree. Prue felt a rush of relief. Life would go on, and it would be good.

At least, the Halliwell line of witches would be practicing white magic, and the world was sure to be a better place for it.

"Awesome," Phoebe said. Kicking that demon's butt back to hell had left her feeling really wired.

"I am so glad that spell worked," Piper said. "Can we go home now?"

"No way! What about Prudence?" Phoebe reminded them.

"That's a good question," Prue said. "We probably have the power to save her, but think about it. If we save her, is it going to screw up the future? I mean, every single one of our ancestors could be affected by this."

A thoughtful look crossed Piper's face as she bit her lower lip. "Phoebe, maybe what's happening to Prudence is what's supposed to be."

"No. No way. I will not accept that. Besides, how do you know we're not *supposed* to save her?" Phoebe argued. "Maybe we were sent back here for a reason—*that* reason." She paused. "I *know* it's right to save Prudence. I can feel it!" Phoebe argued.

"Is that enough?" Piper asked.

"It is for me," Phoebe answered. "And I don't care what either of you say. I'm going to rescue her!"

She thrust her hands deep in the pockets of Prudence's cloak and felt something hard and metallic. Phoebe fished it out. It was the crescent moon, the gold charm that had belonged to Melinda Warren, Prudence's mother. Phoebe pressed it in her hand, wondering how it got in the cloak.

Whooosh!

A vision seeped into her mind. A wet, distorted view of light. Everything wavy and in motion. She was underwater. No. No, she saw *Prudence* underwater, struggling and choking. Oh, no! This was Prudence's own vision of drowning!

But then the wooden chair Prudence was tied to was lifted, and Prudence rose out of the water! She gasped and coughed, then smiled at three familiar faces.

"The Power of Three," Phoebe said aloud.

"Phoebe?" Piper squeezed her hand. "Honey, are you okay?"

When Phoebe related the details of the vision to her sisters, they seemed confused at first.

"With the Power of Three, we can make it happen. Prudence doesn't have to die," Phoebe insisted. "Either way, Cassandra will grow up and have children and pass *The Book of Shadows* on to her daughters. But we can let that little girl have her mom and save someone who's really become a good friend. Please, can you trust me on this one?"

Prue frowned. "I think Phoebe's right," she said. "This fits in with everything we vowed to do. We can't leave here without trying to save Prudence."

"Okay, fine," Piper said, holding up her hands. "So where do you go in town to drown a witch?"

It wasn't difficult to find Prudence. Most of the villagers had gathered at the pond that lay halfway between Prudence's cabin and the center of the village.

Near the edge of the pond a man was hammering at a wooden contraption made of thick beams that connected to a wooden chair.

"We've never had a ducking stool in Salem Village before," he was saying to the man next to him. "But it should serve well for drowning a witch."

Prudence sat in the chair, tied to it by thick ropes. She seemed dazed, almost resigned to her fate. She's probably in shock, Phoebe thought as she pulled the reins on the horse, bumping to a stop.

"Hang toward the back," Prue told her sisters. "Just let things go on as planned."

Phoebe nodded. Let the villagers have their witch-dunking, because when the board came back up, they'd be in for the surprise of their lives.

The man drove one more nail into the

beams. "Done," he said, standing back. "Let the witch meet her fate!"

The crowd cheered as the chair that Prudence sat in was hoisted over the pond.

The man with the waxy face cleared his throat. "Evil must be cleansed from Salem," he proclaimed. "May these waters wash the evil from the witch's soul! Hold her under until she is drowned!"

The crowd cheered again, and the chair with Prudence in it was lowered. Phoebe's heart was in her throat as she watched Prudence's head disappear beneath the slate-gray water.

Then, just as planned, Piper froze time.

The Halliwell sisters hurried to the edge of the pond. Prue leaned over the water and used her powers to raise the stool out of the water and set it back on the shore. A split second later her powers cut through the ropes, freeing a choking, sputtering Prudence.

"Oh, blessed be," she gasped. "It's you."

"Yup." Piper grinned. "I decided to freeze time after all. Just a little later."

Helping Prudence to her feet, Prue explained how they'd taken care of the demon. "And then Phoebe had a vision—"

"Of you coming out of the water," Phoebe interrupted. "I knew it was possible to save you without interrupting the chain of events. But before Piper's freeze ends, you have to get out of here. Pick up Cassandra, ride out of Salem, and never come back."

"Indeed," Prudence said. She climbed into the seat of the cart and bit her lip, holding back tears. "How can I ever thank you—all of you?"

"We should be thanking you," Phoebe said. "You're sort of our grandmother."

"Now go," Prue ordered. "Before someone sees you!"

After a tearful wave, Prudence bolted down the lane. The Charmed Ones watched until she crested a hill and disappeared from sight.

"Whoops," Prue said. "One more detail to take care of." She focused her powers on the empty ducking stool. It rose into the air then sank back into the waters of the pond just as Piper's freeze wore off.

Phoebe stood for a moment to watch the bloodthirsty villagers lift the empty chair from the water.

"The witch is gone!" Wax Man cried.

"Vanished!" added another.

Two men waded into the pond, peering into its murky depths for a trace of Prudence's body. Nothing was there.

"She used her magic to escape!" Wax Man proclaimed. "Is this not proof that she was a witch?"

For once you are right, Phoebe thought with satisfaction.

CHAPTER
19

I hate to rush things, but we'd better get back,"
Piper said. "We stole our teleporting powers
from warlocks. Now that we've gotten rid of
Falcroft, well, the same evil doesn't exist in our
futures. We actually undid it."

Phoebe squinted at her. "Say what?"

"We'll explain later," Prue said. "The thing
is, we'd better get back to San Francisco in the
new millennium while we still can."

They ducked behind an oak tree and formed
a circle. Taking her sisters' hands, Phoebe
watched in wonder as they folded in half over
and over again until they were tiny pieces.
They exploded into tiny star-bursts.

The star-bursts danced momentarily, then
burst into a square piece, which unfolded

177

again and again until the picture of Piper and Prue was complete. Phoebe stared at the wonder of it all when that picture became three-dimensional. Suddenly Piper and Prue were standing on a side street in North Beach about a block away from where they'd been shopping just a few eons ago.

"I can't believe you stole warlocks' powers, you nasty girls," Phoebe said, punching Piper in the shoulder.

"We're really not proud of it," Prue said. "But, actually, I'm a little confused as to whether we did or not. I mean, with the demon gone, *The Book of Shadows* won't have those evil spells in it and we wouldn't have been able to do what we did."

Phoebe held up her hands. "Whatever." It was a deliciously crisp, sunny morning, and she didn't want to waste it on logic.

"You know," Piper said, nudging Prue, "you never did get those boots."

Prue grinned. "Which was exactly what I was thinking when I teleported us back to this spot. Not to mention that Phoebe could use a bit of a makeover. That dress is positively Pilgrim."

"Me?" Phoebe looked from Piper to Prue. "I think we're overlooking that someone here has two black eyes, and another someone is dressed like Vampira."

"So we'll all get makeovers," Piper said, linking arms with her sisters.

"Thanks, guys," Phoebe said. "For everything. I'd be dead in Salem without you, and so would Prudence. I'm so glad we could save her."

"And let's not forget the way that we banished that ugly green demon," Piper added.

Prue licked one finger and checked off an invisible "one" in the air. "One demon down. A few million more to go."

"Count me in," Phoebe said, striding ahead. "Besides, you need me for the Power of Three." Just knowing she was needed for something very important in the here and now made Phoebe smile.

She was one of the Charmed Ones, and that was all that mattered.

About the Author

ROSALIND NOONAN has written more than two dozen books for children and young adults. She has two sisters and likes *Charmed* because of the sister dynamic. She lives in Bayside, New York, and has two children.

Charmed

"We're the protectors of the innocent.
We're known as the Charmed Ones."

–Phoebe Halliwell, "Something Wicca This Way Comes"

Go behind the scenes of television's sexiest supernatural thriller with *The Book of Three*, the *only* fully authorized companion to the witty, witchy world of *Charmed*!

"We all need to believe that magic exists."

–Phoebe Halliwell, "Trial by Magic"

When Phoebe Halliwell returned to San Francisco to live with her older sisters, Prue and Piper, in Halliwell Manor, she had no idea the turn her life—*all* their lives—would take. Because when Phoebe found the Book of Shadows in the Manor's attic, she learned that she and her sisters were the Charmed Ones, the most powerful witches of all time. Battling demons, warlocks, and other black-magic baddies, Piper and Phoebe lost Prue but discovered their long-lost half-Whitelighter, half-witch sister, Paige Matthews. The Power of Three was reborn.

Look for a new Charmed novel every other month!

Published by Simon & Schuster